Mail Order M
A Brides of Beckham Story
Kirsten Osbourne

Copyright © 2021 by Kirsten Osbourne

Unlimited Dreams Publishing

All rights reserved.

Cover design by Erin Dameron Hill/ EDH Graphics

No part of this book may be reproduced in any form or by any electronic or mechanical means including information storage and retrieval systems, without permission in writing from the author. The only exception is by a reviewer, who may quote short excerpts in a review.

This book is a work of fiction. Names, characters, places, and incidents either are products of the author's imagination or are used fictitiously. Any resemblance to actual persons, living or dead, events, or locales is entirely coincidental.

Kirsten Osbourne

Visit my website at www.kirstenandmorganna.com

Printed in the United States of America

Sign up for instant notification of all of Kirsten's New Releases Text 'BOB' to 42828

And

For a complete list of Kirsten's works head to her website wwww.kirstenandmorganna.com

Chapter One

Sydney Weatherby rode through the quiet city of Beckham on her way to the orphanage where she volunteered three mornings per week. She loved riding when the town was so quiet before most people had woken up and gotten their days started. She enjoyed working with the children, and often, all she did was play with them and keep them busy. Today, though, was a day that would be full of chores. It was spring cleaning time, and the orphans were expected to wash windows, scrub floors, and do all the things their mothers would have been doing had they been alive.

Her long blond hair flowed out behind her as she rode, though she knew it was supposed to be in a knot. At least her mother would say it should be in a knot. When she got to the orphanage, she'd brush it and pin it up, so she could escape her mother's wrath.

Her mother hated her habit of riding her bike everywhere, though she'd been the one to get Sydney the bike when she was a girl of twelve. Her mother had been convinced that a bicycle was the answer to the small pudge around Sydney's middle, and her mother had been right! She'd lost all the weight and turned into a beautiful athletic young woman.

But she wouldn't stop riding the bicycle and challenging boys to ride with her. Her mother wasn't happy because she wanted her to flirt with the boys, not best them in bike races. Now she was twenty, and still unmarried, spending her time biking and helping at the orphanage, when her parents wanted her to go to balls and have afternoon teas with potential mothers-in-law. None of that was for Sydney.

An only child, Sydney had been given a boy's name, simply because there wasn't a girl's name picked out. They'd wanted more children, but Sydney, the great disappointment she was, was all they had.

She stopped in front of the orphanage and rested her bike up against the side of the house. Someone would scold her for it later, but for now, it was fine where it was. Sometimes she let the orphans take turns on it and used it as a reward for good behavior.

Walking into the house, she immediately helped make breakfast, though her mother would be scandalized if she realized the woman who ran the orphanage had taught her to cook. Sydney wasn't sure what her mother thought she did with the orphans, but it certainly wasn't cooking and cleaning. Those things were beneath her daughter as far as she was concerned.

As soon as the table was set and food was on the table, Mrs. Anderson, the sweet matron of the home, nodded at Sydney. "Ring the bell."

Sydney walked over to the bell that could be heard throughout the entire house, and took a deep breath, before nodding at Mrs. Anderson. She rang the bell loudly, and then the two of them waited for the onslaught.

It came just as quickly as they expected it to. Children who hadn't eaten in twelve hours came running down the stairs, sliding down the banister, and yelling with excitement.

They all had assigned seats at the table, and each one sat down, obediently bowing their heads for their prayer. "Jimmy, it's your turn to pray," Mrs. Anderson said.

Sydney grinned as she bowed her own head giving it a slight shake. Jimmy's prayers always made her smile.

"Oh, Gracious Heavenly Father, we thank You for this meal You have provided. We also thank You for not allowing Mrs. Anderson to find the puppy Aaron smuggled into the boys' bedroom last night. For helping us get away with stealing penny candies from the mercantile, and for not making it rain today so we can play baseball all day. You truly are a good God. Please help us find a way to get out of doing spring cleaning today because as You know, we like the house messy. It feels like a home that way. In the name of Your son, Christ Jesus, we pray. Amen. And b-women, but don't tell Mrs. Anderson I said b-women. She hates that."

By the time he reached the end, all the orphans were snickering. Sydney turned her back to the table entirely, but she knew the children would see her shoulders shaking. Oh, how she wished her mother would allow her to adopt Jimmy and live in a little house in the country. She'd asked, but her mother said it would be harder to marry her off if she had a child.

When Sydney had pointed out that all the men her mother wanted her to marry were stuffed shirts, her mother had told her she would be marrying, and soon.

Sydney didn't understand why her mother still had so much control over her though. They were a year away from the turning of the century. The Twentieth Century was certain to change the way women were treated, and it couldn't happen soon enough.

Sydney turned back to the table, watching as the orphans all fell on their meal as if they were starving, when in truth, they ate very well for orphans.

Mrs. Anderson stood frowning at Jimmy. He sometimes confessed to things they'd never done in prayers to make her look into something that hadn't happened so they could get away with things that had. And sometimes he told the truth. There was no knowing what he was up to, but he was *always* up to *something*.

Mrs. Anderson handed Sydney the children's assignments for the day, and Sydney obediently read them aloud.

By the time she was done, all the children had sunk low in their seats, and Sydney could tell it was time for her to do something to bolster the spirits. "Jimmy, Aaron, and Howard, we get to wash all the windows outside. That's going to be fun. Whoever washes the most windows—without leaving any spots or streaks—gets to ride my bike for fifteen minutes!"

The three boys lifted their heads, looking excited. "But what about us girls?" Molly, a relatively new orphan, asked. "We have to wash the inside of all the windows and do lots of other things."

Sydney thought about it for a moment. "How about this? I'll have Mrs. Anderson pick the best worker from each of the inside groups, and I'll bestow some sort of reward on you next time I come. I'll try to make the reward fit the child."

Molly looked at Mrs. Anderson, who reluctantly agreed with a nod. "But you must remember that working is done simply to make the house better. Not so you will receive rewards."

Sydney grinned that her idea had been agreed with. If she'd asked Mrs. Anderson earlier, the woman never would have agreed, but by asking in front of the children, she really had no choice.

"Regular chores are done before spring cleaning?" Sydney asked.

"Yes, of course. Dishes must still be done, and the house must still be swept. Nothing can be done until the daily chores are taken care of." Mrs. Anderson couldn't help but smile at the youngest orphan, Agatha, who looked at her with a smile. "Yes, you can help wipe the dishes dry, Agatha."

The next few hours were an absolute whirlwind for the entire household. It was well past two in the afternoon when Sydney noticed the time. She was supposed to be home and dressed for tea by three. Her mother was not going to be pleased.

She hurried to Mrs. Anderson. "I have to go. I need to be dressed for tea at three."

Mrs. Anderson's eyes widened. "There's no way you can make it that quickly!"

"Wish me luck! Maybe you could have Jimmy pray for me," Sydney called back over her shoulder as she threw her leg over her bike and started pedaling for all she was worth.

It was three-twenty when she walked into the parlor for tea with her mother and the potential mother-in-law of the day. Her mother glared at her. "Ah, here is my daughter, Sydney Anne. She's been volunteering at the orphanage."

Sydney nodded, sliding demurely into the seat left for her. "I do apologize for my lateness. I simply lost track of time as I do often when I'm working with the children."

"Sydney, this is Mrs. Sloan. She's one of the Boston Sloans."

Sydney smiled sweetly. Being one of the Boston Sloans must mean something, but Sydney had no idea who the woman was. Probably some banker's wife with a son named something awful like Percival, who couldn't find anyone to marry her uncoordinated unattractive son.

"It's so good to meet you, Mrs. Sloan."

"Tell me about your work at the orphanage," Mrs. Sloan said. "I've always thought about volunteering with orphans, but instead, I just donate old clothes and things my family no longer needs."

"Oh, working with the orphans is such fun!" Sydney said. "Today we were doing spring cleaning, and I had three boys I was supervising as they washed the outside of every window of the orphanage. Mrs. Anderson, the matron, always gives me the three worst behaved boys, because I can get them to do anything. I told the boys whoever washed the most windows without leaving any spots or streaks could ride my bicycle for fifteen minutes, and they all worked as hard as they could."

Mrs. Sloan gaped at Sydney. "You ride a bicycle? In skirts?"

"I wear bloomers underneath my skirts," Sydney said, refusing to back down though her mother was glaring at her.

"If you marry my Percival, you'll have to act like a lady, and that would mean no more bloomers and no more bicycles." From the look in Mrs. Sloan's eyes, Sydney was certain the woman would do something drastic if she wasn't an obedient daughter-in-law. And Sydney had no doubt she would be incapable to obeying the woman.

Sydney tried not to laugh when the man's name really was Percival. "Oh, is that a requirement? I must withdraw my application then."

"Application? This isn't a job you're interviewing for!" Mrs. Sloan glared at her, and then looked at her mother as if to find an ally there.

"Feels like it," Sydney said, getting to her feet. "Don't worry, Mother. I'll see myself out." With that, Sydney went through the kitchen to the side exit of the house. "I'll be back in a few hours."

Mrs. Sanders, the cook, shook her head. "Oh, you've made your mother mad again, haven't you?"

"See you soon!" Sydney felt a twinge of guilt, knowing the servants would be the ones to have to deal with her mother's wrath.

Sydney walked down the street and once again stared up at the Tandy house. Mrs. Tandy sent women to be mail-order brides out west. Even though the west wasn't really known as wild any longer, she knew that many women in the west did real work and didn't flaunt themselves in their very finest every evening trying to make their husbands look better.

She had no desire to marry a stranger, but the idea wasn't as abhorrent as marrying a man who would expect her to be a part of society like her mother did. No, she would instead go to Mrs. Tandy and see if she'd find her a husband. Then she wouldn't have to worry about her mother parading her in front of every suitor from Boston to New York.

Before she lost her nerve, she marched straight up to the house and knocked loudly. It only took a moment for Mr. Tandy to come to the door. He looked surprised to see her but smiled after a moment. "Miss Weatherby, how can I help you today?"

When the Tandys had married, her mother had seen it as terribly scandalous. She didn't feel a woman like Elizabeth should marry her butler. No, in her mother's mind, *no one* should marry their butler.

Though she'd been too young to marry herself, Sydney had silently cheered the couple on.

"Would it be all right if I talked to Mrs. Tandy? My business is of a personal nature." Still wearing the clothes her mother approved of, she felt as if she had to display some semblance of manners. She was going to get an earful when she got home already.

"Of course. Come in." Mr. Tandy gave her a knowing look, and she realized he knew what her business was about. Everyone knew how difficult her mother was, and how progressive Sydney's ideas were. No, he'd understand perfectly.

She followed him down the hall to the last door on the left, which was open, and a blond woman sat at a desk where she was reading something. "Elizabeth? You have a visitor," Mr. Tandy said.

Mrs. Tandy turned to her for a moment, and then smiled. "Come in. Have a seat and tell me what's happening." The two of them had a passing acquaintance, but Mrs. Tandy was different than most of the women who lived on Rock Creek Road, in that she was raised a poor woman, and had become a businesswoman through an act of benevolence.

Sydney moved to the sofa, while Mr. Tandy said he would get tea for them. Sydney wanted to tell the man she was chockful of tea and good manners, but she restrained herself.

"My mother is determined for me to marry a man with a high place in society. I'm determined to wear bloomers in public and ride my bicycle wherever I please. One of us is going to end up miserable, and as it's my life, I'd rather it wasn't me."

Mrs. Tandy nodded. "So, you're considering becoming a mail-order bride and would like me to assist you?"

"Exactly." Sydney couldn't back down now. She had to go through with it or let her mother have her way, in which case she may as well jump off the tallest building in town. No man with a high place in society would ever allow his wife to go about in bloomers.

"I just received this letter. Now the man sending it hasn't been as thoroughly investigated as usual, but my husband has placed some telegrams and gotten a good response. Would you like to read the letter?"

Sydney nodded, anxious to see what kind of man Elizabeth saw for her. "I would."

As soon as she had the letter, Sydney read through it slowly, a slow smile coming to her face.

To whom it may concern:

I'm looking for an unusual woman. One who wouldn't be embarrassed to wear bloomers in public. One who is not afraid to do things most society women wouldn't. I have a house in Fort Worth, Texas, and I would welcome a woman who is willing to work. No woman who thinks life should be a bed of roses need apply.

Pay your own way to Fort Worth, and I will take care of the rest of your expenses. I look forward to meeting you. I'm a well-known businessman, so all you need to do is ask for me once you are off the train.

Sincerely,

Randy Ranch

After reading the letter a second and third time, Sydney nodded. "I do believe this is the man for me. He sounds like he has no worries about his wife being a perfect lady, and that's the main thing I'm trying to avoid."

The tea came then, and Mrs. Tandy offered some cookies. "If you are certain, you may do it, and I won't send any other ladies."

Sydney nodded. "I'll need to say goodbye to the orphans, but I may not bother to tell my mother. We all know she won't be pleased, though I think my father might be. He's tired of her constant nagging about me getting a good husband."

"I think it is safe to say that good is in the eye of the beholder, don't you?"

"I do! I'll leave Monday." It was just Friday, so she would have a couple of days to pack her things and go. "Would you be willing to send my belongings on to me? I'll only take my bicycle and a small carpet bag on the train."

"Oh, happily. Bring them to me, and I'll send them in care of my sister, Susan. She lives outside Fort Worth with her husband and children."

"What's her last name now? Perhaps I could look her up while I'm there."

"I think that would be lovely. Her married name is Dailey."

Sydney got to her feet and shook Elizabeth's hand. "Thank you so much."

"Just remember, if he ever hurts you in any way, you shouldn't stay. You should come home or go straight to my sister who will help you."

"I won't forget." As Sydney left the Tandy house, she felt as if she had a new lease on life. She was going to be happy despite her mother's machinations.

Chapter Two

True to her word, Sydney packed up her belongings and bribed some servants to take them to the Tandys' home. On Saturday morning, she rode out to the orphanage on the other end of town and brought prizes for the children who had earned them. She brought three of her old dolls, and several coins for the boys. After distributing prizes, she went to Mrs. Anderson and whispered what she was about to do. The other woman looked worried, but she understood why Sydney felt as if she must do it. How could she not?

Sydney was the model daughter all weekend, attending two balls, and having tea with two potential mothers-in-law. She acted like the daughter her mother had always wanted, instead of herself.

Instead of long, tear filled goodbyes, Sydney wrote a short note to her father, whom she was certain would understand why she was leaving. He'd always been an ally of sorts. "I have gone west to marry. I will send you and mother a letter when I am settled into my new home. I do ask that you not tell mother for at least a week that you know what I've done. I do not want to marry the kind of man mother is determined for me to marry. I will be good. Love, Sydney."

She left the note on his desk for him to find the following morning. There was a train that left Beckham at six every morning, heading west, and she planned to be on it. She'd switch trains as she needed to, contemplating and then discarding the idea of traveling to California and seeing the entire country from her own private sleeping car, but she realized it wasn't a good idea. No, she'd stick with the original plan and marry Randy Ranch.

Fort Worth, Texas sounded like the wild west anyway.

DAYS LATER, SYDNEY arrived in Fort Worth, Texas, tired and dirty. It had been a long train ride, and she was ready to just sleep in a bed that didn't make sounds. She'd thought the train was a great adventure until she'd gotten on it, and the adventure had worn off within an hour. No, Fort Worth would have to be her home because she was not getting on that thing again.

She got her bicycle from the luggage car and picked up her carpet bag. Now she must find Mr. Randy Ranch.

As she wandered away from the train station, she realized she was not in a good part of town. She got onto her bike and turned around, heading north instead of south. The buildings and houses there seemed to be in better order.

She stopped at the first business she saw, a general store, and she wandered inside. "Hello. I'm looking for Randy Ranch." Sydney was dressed in bloomers and pushing her bicycle. The woman behind the counter looked her up and down.

"You looking for the man or the house?"

"I don't know what the house is. No, I'm looking for the man."

The woman scratched her head. "Well, he owns all the businesses on this block, but he doesn't often make an appearance. Mr. Ranch is an important man."

"Can you tell me where I might find him then?" Sydney asked. She wasn't sure what was so complicated about finding the man if he was as prominent as it seemed.

"He's probably at the house."

"What house?" Sydney asked, growing a little more confused by the moment.

"The brothel...Randy's Ranch."

Sydney stared at the woman for a moment. "Brothel? This man owns a brothel?" How could she have come this far to marry a brothel-owner? No, she had to figure out how to change things.

"He does. Is that not the man you're looking for?"

"No, I don't believe it is. Could you perchance tell me how I might find Mrs. Susan Dailey?"

"The Daily Ranch is a few miles outside of town."

"That's all right. I brought my bicycle." Though she was tired and had hoped to sleep immediately, it obviously wasn't going to happen.

The woman made her a map, explaining where to turn.

Sydney thanked her. "May I have a glass of water before I head out there? It's hot."

The woman smiled. "It's only April. Wait until July."

"I think I'd rather not," Sydney said with a grin. She wasn't certain she would be able to survive the heat of the summer if it was this hot in April!

The woman gave her a glass of water and Sydney gave her a silver dollar for her trouble. "I thank you for taking the time to help me."

"But...this is a day's wage!"

"That's all right. The help is appreciated." Sydney handed the empty glass back to the other woman and set out on her bike in the direction the woman had indicated. She wouldn't be sleeping in a brothel or with a brothel owner that night.

Just as she thought she'd gone too far, she saw the street the woman had said to turn on. From there she was on empty roads with fields as far as the eye could see. It was interesting to see the difference between Massachusetts and Texas.

It took her half an hour to reach the ranch, and she was thrilled when it came into view. She could see the stable, much larger than the barn, next to the blue house she'd been told Mrs. Dailey lived in.

She rested her bike against the stairs for the front porch and climbed them, knocking on the door.

The woman who answered the door was older, more her grandmother's age than Mrs. Tandy's. "I'm looking for Mrs. Susan Dailey?"

"Yes, of course." The women gave her bicycle a strange look, but then she opened the door wide. "If you'll wait in the parlor."

Sydney gratefully sat in the chair indicated by the woman and closed her eyes for a moment. She was used to riding long distances but not in the heat. That heat felt as if it was the very hottest day of summer. It was brutal.

Sydney wasn't certain how long she sat there before she opened her eyes, looking around her. A woman who was much closer to Mrs. Tandy's age sat with a little girl on her lap, watching her sleep.

"I'm so sorry! I didn't mean to fall asleep."

Mrs. Dailey smiled, nodding. "I don't mind. Could you tell me who you are?"

Sydney burst into laughter. "I suppose that information would help. My name is Sydney Weatherby, and I was sent to Fort Worth by your sister, Elizabeth."

"Now you're starting to make sense."

"I came here to marry a Randy Ranch, but when I arrived, I found out he was a brothel owner, and I'm not even supposed to know what a brothel is!"

"Oh my! Well, Mr. Ranch owns a good portion of Fort Worth. You don't want to marry him. He spends more time in his own businesses, including the Red Door Saloon and Gambling Establishment than he should." Mrs. Dailey shook her head. "So, do you want to stay here and find a husband with me, or do you want to take that long train ride back to Beckham?"

"You'd let me stay?" Sydney was shocked at the offer.

"Well, sure. My sister sent you here, so I'll help out. We have room, now that our two oldest boys have moved out. The oldest is even married!"

"Well, maybe you should introduce me to your second oldest then," Sydney said, joking.

"That's not a bad idea!" Mrs. Dailey said. "You're sure pretty, and looking at your bloomers, I'd say you like adventure."

"I do! I enjoy riding my bicycle more than anything. I was joking about you introducing your son, though I would like to stay. I can pay room and board." Sydney had always saved the money she'd been given by her parents for ribbons for her hair. She had enough ribbons! Who on earth needed to buy more?

"There's no need for that. You just meet people and see what you see. It'll be fun to have another Beckham woman around. Do you know Alice Miller?"

Sydney thought for a moment and then remembered a girl who had worked for the mercantile back in Beckham. "Oh, sure! Everyone knows Alice."

"She's married to my oldest son, so there will be three of us Beckham ladies here."

"Wait...I thought Alice and Mrs. Tandy were sisters?"

"Oh, they are."

"And you and Elizabeth are sisters?"

Mrs. Dailey looked highly amused at the confusion on Sydney's face. "My four oldest are sons by marriage."

Sydney nodded. "I'm so glad to hear that!" She'd been picturing not so nice things until that information was shared.

"You need to call me Susan. Let me show you to the room you can use, and I'll let Mrs. Hackenshleimer know you're staying here."

"Is that who answered the door?"

Susan nodded. "Yes, she came with the house, husband and four oldest sons. She's our housekeeper."

"I see. Well, I'm thrilled to meet her too. Texas is hot."

"Yes, it is! I miss colder weather only in the summers though." Susan got to her feet. "We have a couple of hours before supper if you want to nap or bathe. And don't worry, we don't dress for supper, and your bloomers won't be a problem at all."

"Thank you, Susan. I appreciate your hospitality." Sydney was surprised at how a kind person could turn a dreadful day into a good one. Perhaps it was the entire Miller family who could do so. She knew Elizabeth had, and Alice had been kind to her at the store where she worked.

"We'll send Elizabeth a telegram letting her know you're all right."

"Tell her it's not time to tell my parents yet, please."

Susan grinned. "Your parents don't know you're here?"

"No, and until I'm married, it would be best if they didn't." Sydney sighed, wishing her mother didn't have to worry, but she would not be returning to Beckham. Not ever.

"I understand. Elizabeth has helped several young women under similar circumstances."

"Thank you for being willing to take me in. I could stay in a boarding house or something if you'd rather…and can show me where a boarding house is."

"That's what I did when I first arrived. But no, stay here. It'll be fun."

Sydney smiled. "I appreciate your hospitality. I think I will sleep. And I'll bathe after supper if that's not too much trouble."

"Not at all." Susan led Sydney up the stairs, and to a door to the left at the top of the stairs. "This will be your bedroom for now. I'll send one of the boys to wake you for supper. Is there anything you want now?"

"A glass of water would make me the happiest woman alive!"

"Give me a minute, and I will ensure your happiness."

With that, Susan left. Sydney looked around the small room, unpacking her carpet bag. There wouldn't be enough room for her clothes when they arrived, but there was enough for what she had at the moment.

She pulled back the covers to get ready to sleep as soon as she'd had her water. A knock at the door had her opening it to a young pregnant woman. "I'm Alice. I remember you shopping at the store in Beckham with your mother!" She handed Sydney a drink of water.

Sydney drained it before thanking her. "I appreciate that so much. The Texas heat is awful."

"It is. Glad to see you here. Susan explained what happened. You should marry my brother-in-law, Lewis. He's been talking for a while about sending off for a bride."

Sydney frowned. "Not sure I could do that, now that I can see it almost got me into some big trouble."

"Lewis is a good man. Susan and I'll work on you!"

Sydney laughed. "I'll meet him, but I'm not promising to marry him!"

"That's good. Because we're not looking for a promise." Alice smiled sweetly. "My husband, Albert and I, our daughter, and Lewis are all coming to dinner tonight. We want to give you a proper welcome! So glad you're here."

"Me too! You don't ride a bike by any chance, do you?"

Alice looked down at her swollen middle. "I'm not so sure that would be a good idea right now."

Sydney grinned. "I'll teach you after the baby is born."

"That sounds like fun to me. I remember always seeing you ride up and down the street in front of the store. You look so free when you ride. And you're faster than all the boys."

"That was my favorite part, I'm afraid..."

Alice laughed. "It would have been mine too. I can't ride a bike, but I can outshoot all the boys."

"Sounds like we have skills to trade!" Sydney hid a yawn behind her hand.

"Oh, I'm so sorry! Susan said you were about to nap. I'll go, let you sleep, and I'll see you at supper. I can't wait to get to know you better!"

Sydney smiled. "We were never friends in Beckham, and I come here, and we're going to be best friends, aren't we?"

"I sure hope so!" Alice replied. "And sisters-in-law if I have my way!"

Sydney shook her head as her new friend walked toward the top of the stairs, closing her door. Sleep was all she cared about.

She undressed to her bloomers and corset, untied the strings of her corset, and collapsed onto the bed. It was soft, but not cloyingly soft like her bed in Beckham. The window was open and a nice breeze was coming through the room. She was going to like Texas. There was no doubt in her mind about that.

As she drifted off to sleep, she thought about how horrid her life would have been if she'd married the owner of a brothel who spent all his time in it. Maybe jumping on a train and taking off across the country wasn't the smartest thing she'd ever done.

But staying in Beckham and marrying her mother's choice of beaus would have been the absolute worst thing she'd ever done in her entire life. She was glad she'd left, even if she had narrowly escaped a bad situation.

She was in the arms of a loving family now, and they would treat her right. She could feel it with everything inside her. Thank goodness she'd asked Mrs. Tandy for Susan's last name. She shuddered thinking about how her life could have turned out if she hadn't asked one simple question.

Sleep took a while in coming after those dreadful thoughts. But once she was asleep, it was all over. It was a quiet dreamless sleep. Well, sort of. She dreamed she was sleeping beside a too hot fireplace, but it was better than where her dreams could have gone.

Chapter Three

When she was woken for supper that evening, Sydney immediately got up and washed her face and hands with the pitcher and bowl in the corner of her room. Someone must have filled it while she slept, which told her she'd slept a great deal harder than she'd thought. The words, "Like a rock," came to mind. She was usually a light sleeper, but she was very comfortable with the Dailey family.

She went down the stairs, listening to the sounds of laughter. She knew it would be easy to always find the family. They were apparently loud when they were all together.

When she reached the sound of the voices, she found them all in a large sitting room, all of them casually dressed. As soon as she entered the room, Susan walked to her side. "This is Sydney, who came here as a mail-order bride," she said, smiling.

Two young men who looked identical looked at another young man. "Don't look at me!" the man being looked at said. "I thought about sending for a mail-order bride, but I didn't actually do it. I was half-afraid Aunt Elizabeth was going to send me a member of the demon horde like she did Albert!"

Sydney smiled. Lewis. *That has to be Lewis.* Then her eyes widened. "Wait...your family was known as the demon horde?" Sydney asked Susan. "I knew it was a local farmer's children, but no one ever said it was the Millers. You're practically famous in Beckham!"

Alice stood to one side. "Famous? Don't you mean infamous?" she asked, picking up a little girl and holding her close. "We'll eat soon, Rachel."

Rachel rested her head on her mama's shoulder. She couldn't have been more than eighteen months old.

Susan frowned. "Are you trying to starve my niece-granddaughter?"

Alice nodded. "Yes, she hasn't ever been fed. See how she's wasting away to nothing?"

Everyone laughed at that. The little girl was more than a little chubby, and as cute as could be.

Mrs. Hackenschleimer stepped into the room then. "Supper's on the table."

Not knowing where the dining room was, Sydney followed along behind the family. She was hungrier than she'd realized. She could smell delicious food filling the air. "Something smells wonderful!"

"Fried chicken and mashed potatoes," Lewis said, leaning close. "It's what she always serves first-time guests. Her fried chicken is worth crossing the country for."

"Well, then I'll be certain to get a big piece," Sydney said, wanting to study the man, but also not wanting to be rude. So far, everyone had assumed she was there to marry him. Perhaps he was a good candidate for a possible husband.

He was seated across from her at the table, and Sydney was glad. She could watch how he interacted with family as well as have a chance to really look at him and not be considered rude.

The identical young men were on either side of him, but they looked as if they were a little too young to marry her. Perhaps seventeen or eighteen? Sydney couldn't help but wonder if they were Susan's children or some that were hers by marriage, like Lewis and Albert.

Susan sat at the foot of the table with David at the head. Once David had prayed over the meal, Susan introduced her to each of the people at the table. She had been right about Lewis, and she quickly discovered that the twins were Susan's stepsons, though they both called her Ma and seemed to think of her as their mother.

"How many children do you have?" Sydney finally asked.

"David has ten. I've given birth to six of them, but I think of all of them as my children." Susan looked down the table at Lewis. "Even the two pranksters."

"Wait...are Albert and Lewis the pranksters?" Sydney asked, her eyes wide.

"They are."

"But...how could you let a member of the demon horde marry a prankster?" Sydney looked at little Rachel, half expecting to see horns pop out of the girl's hair.

"I didn't know Elizabeth had sent another of our sisters. Alice was only five when I left Beckham, and the three of them, Albert, Alice, and Lewis, conspired against me, not telling me that Alice was my sister. They even made up a fake last name for her!" Susan looked at the three of them, and not one of them looked guilty. They instead looked awfully pleased with themselves.

"What a way to greet a sister you haven't seen in fifteen years!" Sydney shook her head. "Your family's pranks were considered epic tales of fun by most of the children around Beckham. None of the churches would let the children go there very long. Usually within a month, the pastor would take the parents aside and tell them their children are corruptive influences on the rest of the young men and women in the church."

Alice nodded. "We never did last longer than a couple of months at a church. We scared lots of teachers away too. Now the school board will only hire men, and the men need to be willing to *not* spare the rod."

"You must have gone to the country school south of town?"

Susan frowned. "We did. The four oldest children in my family were always well behaved because Ma and Pa would switch us if we weren't. By the time Alice came around, Ma was so tired trying to deal with so many kids, there was no discipline at all unless it was either Elizabeth or me dishing it out."

"I truly feel like I'm in the midst of greatness."

Susan sighed. "I got away from all the younger siblings, and then married David to find myself the mother of two just like those siblings." She shook her head. "You'd think I was doing something to attract them all, but I really wasn't."

"I can't believe you went through with the marriage when they were so ill-behaved."

"I guess you should hear the whole story of my marriage," Susan said, taking a bite of her chicken before continuing. "I came here to marry David's brother, but he was killed in a shoot-out in Hell's Half Acre before I arrived."

"What is Hell's Half Acre?" Sydney asked, confused.

"It's the bad part of town south of the railroad station where you came into town," Lewis said. "You should never go there. It's not safe. Why even Butch Cassidy has been spotted there."

"I was there today! I got frightened and turned to walk back toward the railroad station, and I didn't stop until I was in an area that didn't look so run down," Sydney said, feeling like the world's biggest idiot. "As you were saying, Susan?"

"Yes, so my fiancé was killed, so David met me at the station, telling me what happened but offering to marry me instead. He told me he was a widower with four children. I insisted on having supper with the family so I could see how his children behaved before I would agree, not wanting to be saddled with children just like my brothers and sisters. So, David *paid* Albert and Lewis to behave, hoping I'd marry him if they weren't as ill-behaved as normal."

Sydney's jaw dropped, and she turned to look at David, pointing with her fork. "You did that?"

David just smirked at her, raising one shoulder in a shrug.

"He did that," Susan said. "Within minutes of the wedding being over, the boys were acting as they usually did though, and I knew. I was so furious with the man, but I'd already spoken my words, and I wasn't about to go home. Not with the demon horde waiting there for me."

"That's terrible!" Sydney couldn't believe these two were still married, and they had six children.

Lewis grinned at her. "We tried to behave...sometimes."

"I'm not sure how I feel about this. I mean, the story is funny, but how can I trust any of you?"

Alice smiled. "Susan and I will always tell you the truth. Don't worry about the others."

Sydney sat back in her chair, carefully cutting a bite of chicken from the breast she'd selected. Everyone stared at her as she took her first bite. "Oh, it's good!"

"Do you always eat fried chicken with a knife and fork?" Susan asked, helping Sydney to understand what the looks were about.

"I don't know that I've ever had fried chicken," Sydney said. "My mother has never liked chicken, so it was never served."

Alice grinned. "Your mother is the sort who probably would eat it with a knife and fork. Most people just pick it up and bite in, though. It's one of those foods that is fine to eat with your fingers."

Sydney picked up the chicken for her second bite and just bit right into it. "You're right. It tastes much better this way! I wonder if I would like spinach if I ate it with my fingers."

"No, you wouldn't," Alice said, making a face.

After supper, Sydney stood and offered to help with the dishes, but Susan refused. "You just got here! Why don't you go for a nice walk? I'm sure Lewis wouldn't mind accompanying you. There are wild animals around, so it doesn't make sense to go alone."

Despite the fact that she knew Susan was trying to get her to marry her second stepson, Sydney agreed. "That sounds enjoyable. Perhaps he can tell me about the ranch."

Lewis got to his feet and offered Sydney his arm, ignoring the giggles of his younger siblings. "Yes, let's go for a walk."

As soon as they were out of the house, Lewis started talking about the operations of the ranch. "We run some cattle, but we've never had a huge number here. Albert is the cattle rancher in the family. Pa breeds and trains horses. If a local rancher needs a horse broken, he'll bring it to Pa, but the majority of his work is done on the horses we breed here on the ranch. I oversee the breeding, and Pa does the training. My younger brothers, the twins, are learning to train them as well as Pa. Takes some of the work off Pa's shoulders."

"Do you enjoy breeding horses?" Back east the question would have been considered indelicate. Here? It seemed to come out of her mouth naturally.

"I do. We have one of the best studs around, and we're always buying mares. I actually ride out to different ranches around, seeing what the quality of their mares is, and I bring a lot home. That's my part in the whole thing. Then I choose which mares are bred when. I've got my eye on another stud, but we're trying to decide if it's worth the price."

"That sounds interesting. When you ride out to places, do you go on a horse or on a bicycle?" she asked.

He looked at her for a moment. "A horse. A horse breeder who goes everywhere on a bicycle would be frowned on, don't you think?"

"Probably. I just happen to love riding my bicycle, and I wondered if you rode too." It occurred to her that it would be a wonderful courting activity, riding bicycles together. There were even bicycles built for two they could share the work of pedaling on. It sounded like a great deal of fun to her.

Lewis leaned against a fence, both of his forearms against the wood. "I've never tried. I don't have a problem with bicycles, but horses are more convenient around here."

"I can understand that. How do you feel about women who wear bloomers and ride bicycles?" she asked. If it was something that bothered him, there would be no reason to set her cap for him. None at all.

"I think women should wear what's comfortable for them. Susan wears split skirts when she rides, and so does Alice. They just work better with the horses. I've seen horses get spooked by a skirt and almost kill a woman who was trying to mount it. So, I think bloomers should be worn on horses as well. And I think women should do things for fun and not always work. I don't think Susan remembers what fun is. She thinks it's relaxing to have several women over for tea, and then all of them do their mending together."

"Oh, trust me. I always have fun." She glanced over at him in the waning sunlight. "Are you looking for a wife?" She'd found she preferred straightforward questions. She would never know if she didn't ask.

"I haven't really been looking, but I'm not averse to the idea either. Say if a woman who was supposed to marry someone else came into town, realized the man was not suitable for her to marry, well then, I might be interested."

Sydney grinned. "I see. How would you know if you were interested? Or more importantly how would the young lady in question know if you were interested?" She was finding herself more and more enamored of the man by the moment. When everyone had started telling her she needed to marry Lewis, she'd thought they were just being silly, or trying to get her to marry an undesirable man. Now she knew he was a truly viable option.

"Well, I guess if the woman appealed to me physically, then I'd try to get to know her a little better. I don't want to marry a woman who thinks it's my job to keep the house, or thinks she needs to constantly have a servant working for her. Albert had a crush on a woman like that for a while, and neither of us wanting to marry a woman who would sit around reading dime novels all day instead of working."

"And once you got to know her some? How would you let her know you were interested in a little more than just a casual acquaintance?" she persisted.

"Well, I think I'd probably take her waist in my hands, like so," he said, putting his words to action. "And then I'd probably try to steal a kiss." When his lips pressed against hers, she felt a shiver run up her spine. Many men had stolen kisses from her, but they all bored her. Not Lewis.

Once he raised his head, she looked at him, wondering what would happen next. "I see."

"Then I'd tell my ma that I wanted to know everything about the girl, and she'd figure out how to find that stuff out. Probably by asking the girl herself."

"That makes sense."

"And then I'd have her over for supper, and let my Pa and Susan tell me what they thought of her after. In my experience, when you marry, you marry the whole family, and not just one person. But once I found out that they liked her, I may just propose that fast. I don't see a need for grass to grow under my feet."

"We should probably head inside," Sydney said softly. She was still so tired from her journey. "I'll be curious to know what your parents thought of me."

"Me too."

Once they reached the house, Sydney sought out Susan and bid her goodnight. She was too tired to stay up much longer. "I promise I won't sleep this much tomorrow," she said with a laugh.

Susan shook her head. "It's going to take a few days for you to recover from that journey."

"I hope you're wrong, and I'm at full strength tomorrow. I want to help with the chores."

"I'd like that a lot. Goodnight, Sydney."

"Goodnight, Susan." Sydney turned to David and then to Lewis, both of whom were right there. "Goodnight, gentleman. I'll see you tomorrow." With that, she went upstairs to find the comfortable bed she'd napped on for so long. A bath could wait until morning.

Chapter Four

Sydney realized when she woke just before noon the following day that Susan had been right. It was going to take her a few days to recover from the long journey, followed by the bicycle ride in such a hot and humid climate.

She had lunch with Susan and Alice, who had decided to join them, and the children who were not yet in school.

The topic of conversation didn't turn to Lewis. It started and ended there. "What did you think of Lewis?" Alice asked. "Isn't he a handsome, kind man?"

"He was very nice," Sydney replied. She didn't want to say too much with his mother and sister-in-law sitting right there.

Susan grinned. "He was certainly infatuated with you. He asked what his father and I think of you, and we told him we would readily approve of a courtship."

"We haven't discussed that yet." Not outright. She'd asked, and he'd given her most of an answer, but she was waiting to see him again before she really knew anything.

"Well, you should!" Alice said. "I understand your parents don't know you're here?"

"They don't. If they did, my mother would have a man here taking me home to Beckham, whether I was kicking and screaming or not. I told my father what I was doing in a note but asked him not to tell my mother until I'd been gone for a full week. I was afraid she would find me somehow and force me to marry a boar...or a bore." Sydney spelled both of the homonyms out so the others would know what she meant.

Susan and Alice both laughed. "I would think that means you need to marry quickly, though, doesn't it?" Alice asked, not willing to give up the subject.

"You're like a dog with a bone!" Sydney said. "Yes, it would be best if I married quickly. I do worry my parents will find me here."

"I think Lewis is a good choice," Alice said.

"As do I," Susan echoed her younger sister.

"I like him fine, but I'm certainly not in love with him."

"That comes with time," the two sisters said in unison. All of them laughed.

"You both say that because you were mail-order brides and initially your marriages were loveless."

Susan sighed. "You came here to *be* a mail-order bride. Why not at least consider Lewis? I promise you he's as well-trained as I could manage, and he rarely pees on the ceiling in the bathroom anymore."

Sydney let out a bark of laughter. "Did he do that when he was young?"

Susan nodded. "He once even asked my husband to paint a target on the ceiling, and David considered it! Until they talked to me of course." I woke up a sleeping baby when I read this!

"I'm glad you were able to talk some sense into them," Sydney said. "It sounds like he's been a difficult child."

Susan shrugged. "I thought my life was over when I realized what Albert and Lewis were really like. But I got to know them and grew to love them both quickly. They were definitely no worse than Alice was."

Alice gave her sister her best innocent look. "I never tried to pee on the ceiling, though."

Susan simply shook her head.

"If Lewis wants to court me, I'm more than willing."

"Just stay open-minded about it," Susan said. "You need to marry, and he's available, and I know he's attracted to you."

"That's true..."

Alice nodded enthusiastically. "Yes, give him a chance. You two should come over for supper tonight!" She clapped her hands together excitedly. "I'll make chicken and dumplings, and we'll all talk. I want to get to know you better too. You're my new best friend whether we like it or not."

Sydney smiled. "I think we both like it."

Alice grinned. "Yes, we do!"

After their lunch, Sydney looked around the house to see if anything needed done, but she saw nothing. "I'd be happy to help with anything you need. Would you like me to do some laundry? Wash windows? Scrub floors? I know how!"

Susan and Alice exchanged a glance.

"What?" Sydney asked, needing to understand the silent communication between the sisters.

Alice answered for them both. "Only a woman who has grown up in a wealthy family would brag they knew how to clean. Susan and I were both cleaning every day from the day we were old enough to drag a kitchen chair to the basin so we could wash and wipe the dishes dry."

Sydney felt strange all at once. "My mother didn't allow me to clean. She said it was servants' work. But I worked at the orphanage outside of town, and I learned how to cook and clean there. And I learned a lot about children." She couldn't cook a lot of meals, but the ones she did know how to make, she made well.

"Do you want children?" Susan asked.

Sydney shrugged. "I do want them. I wanted to adopt one of the boys at the orphanage, but I would have needed my mother's permission, and she was afraid it would keep me from finding the husband she wanted for me."

"Your mother sounds perfectly awful," Susan said.

Alice nodded. "Oh, she was. She was always telling Sydney what she should and shouldn't do. I was stocking shelves at the store one day, and I heard her give Sydney a whole lecture on how she was to sit when someone was over for tea. It lasted for more than twenty minutes! I was ready to stick cotton in my ears, so I didn't have to hear another word of it."

Sydney shrugged. "I remember when she did that. She lectured me about everything from asking boys to race bicycles with me to telling me ladies don't spit in public. I didn't listen very often."

Alice blinked. "Did you spit in public?"

"Never! But I told my mother I liked to spit in public to get a rise out of her. She was very vocal about what was right and wrong for a lady to do. Her favorite was, 'A lady must never touch a man she's not married to. Not even when dancing with them.' How am I supposed to waltz with a man if I can't touch him? She never would answer that question."

"Did she allow you to waltz with men?"

"If they were suitable in her eyes she did." Alice groaned. "I cannot bear the thought of going back to Beckham and being under her rule again. I would simply rather die!"

Susan shook her head. "That's a little too dramatic. No, you should not go back to Beckham. I think you should marry Lewis. I'll insist."

"I won't have a man who is forced to marry me. We'll work it out."

At that point there was a loud knock on the door. A man stood with a huge trunk and a letter for Susan.

Susan eyed the trunk, but quickly opened the letter. "This is from Elizabeth. She told me to find you so I can give you this." Looking at the trunk once more, Susan's eyes met Sydney's. "All those clothes are not going to fit in your small room."

"Lewis has more room at his house," Alice said, once again bringing the conversation back to Lewis. It seemed that it would be impossible to talk of anything else with Susan and Alice around.

"I won't unpack them all," Sydney said. "But I may unpack all my bloomers. Since no one has seemed shocked by them yet, I think I'll wear them all the time."

Susan grinned. "You should. I don't care if anyone is bothered by them. They look so terribly comfortable."

"They are!" Sydney insisted. "I love wearing them so much. Especially when I ride my bicycle."

"You'll teach me to ride it after the baby comes?" Alice asked, looking toward the front door as if she was trying to catch another peek at the strange contraption.

"Of course I will. It's really easy."

Alice looked at Susan. "What about you? Are you going to learn?"

Susan shook her head. "I'd like to, but I can't risk being injured."

Alice's jaw dropped. "You're pregnant again, aren't you?"

Susan frowned. "I thought I was too old for more babies after three years without conceiving, but apparently I was *wrong*."

Sydney smiled. "That's wonderful news!"

"Says the woman with no children," Susan said. "This will give me eleven children. Eleven!"

"Sounds like a good start to me," Sydney replied. She was mostly joking, but she loved children. The orphanage had been her favorite place to be, and she'd sneaked away to go there every time she could get away with it.

"Oh, Lord. She even speaks like Lewis does about children."

"He wants a lot?" Sydney asked, wanting to know so much more about Lewis without asking outright. She didn't want them to know she was interested in him because they would redouble their efforts to get her and Lewis married off then.

Alice nodded. "He wants an even dozen at least. That's what he says anyway."

"Do you want a lot of children, Alice?" Sydney tried again to steer the subject away from her and Lewis.

"I'd like several. Right after Rachel was born, I decided no more, but I can't keep to that." Alice shrugged. "And apparently my husband and I can't keep our hands to ourselves, so there will be more babies."

Susan nodded. "Just like his father. I'm sure Lewis will be similar."

"I guess it's nice knowing they don't stray when looking for affections," Sydney said.

After clearing the table together, Susan sent Sydney home with Alice. "Show her your house, and you two have some fun while the baby naps."

Alice nodded. "Absolutely. Come see my house."

Sydney didn't argue. Instead, she followed her friend out the door and toward another part of the ranch. "Do you live on the same ranch?"

Alice shook her head. "No, but we live on an adjacent property. Albert is buying up as much property as he can so we can run more cattle. Our herd is already one of the biggest in the area, but he tells me we need more. I'm just glad I'm not the one having to build all the fences and do the real work. It's nice to just stay at home and do the housework and cook."

"Tell me about chicken and dumplings," Sydney said. "I've seen them, but never eaten them. Are they as good as the orphans said they were?"

Alice frowned. "Your mother not eating chicken has really made you miss out on some awfully tasty food."

"I guess it has."

Alice described chicken and dumplings to Sydney, and Sydney was excited to try them. "I can't wait!"

"I'll make a cake as well. Everyone loves cakes."

"I do love cakes." Her mother had been against her eating sweets as well. She'd always been worried she'd gain weight.

"Then we'll have one." They walked some distance before Alice opened the door to a small house. "This is my house."

Sydney stepped inside to find a house perfectly in order. There didn't seem to be a speck of dirt anywhere. "Is your house always this clean?" she asked, trying to look in every direction at once.

Alice grinned. "I don't have enough children to keep me terribly busy yet, so I clean. It keeps me doing something. When I finish cleaning, I head over to Susan's, and we spend the rest of the day sewing, or I help her with her chores. Being a housewife is rather lonely work."

"But it's good here because you have each other? I'm starting to understand why you want me to marry Lewis so badly. You want another friend around."

"Another sister," Alice said with a smile. "I do think you and Lewis will be good together though. Did he kiss you?"

Sydney blushed. "What kind of question is that?"

"One that doesn't need to be answered now that I see your blush. Tell me, did it make your toes curl?"

For a moment, Sydney considered denying it, but she decided she wanted the other woman's advice too much. "It did. Is that normal?"

Alice laughed. "It's normal when it's the right man. Right after we were married a man decided he wanted me instead of his own wife. Long story, but he tried to kiss me. I wanted to vomit because the very thought of him kissing me made me sick to my stomach. Albert is the right man, without a doubt."

"And because my toes curled, Lewis is the right man?"

"I think so. You need to see if you can stand to be in one another's presence of course, but failing hostility between you, I'd say he's the man you should marry."

"I will think on that. Thanks for being honest with me."

"No problem. We're best friends, remember? You can ask me anything."

"I will probably take you up on that. Not right now, though. I want to see the rest of this house of yours."

"Rachel fell asleep on the way home. I'm going to put her in her bed, and then we'll look around some more. She'll nap for a good hour or two while I start supper. I'll teach you to make my chicken and dumplings. They're even better than Susan's."

"Are Susan's any good?"

"They're fabulous. But mine are better."

Sydney smiled at the other woman's confidence in her cooking. "Then I need to learn from the best, don't I?"

It would have never occurred to Sydney that cooking with a friend would be fun, but she and Alice laughed most of the afternoon as Sydney tried her hand at cutting dumplings for the first time. It was truly a joyful day, very different than one she'd be having in Beckham.

Sydney owed a huge debt to the Miller family for not only sending her to Fort Worth, but for giving her a place to live and people to have fun with. She was very thankful she'd gotten up the nerves to knock on Elizabeth's door. She didn't yet know what being a bride would be like, but she certainly loved the sisters she'd come into contact with.

For once, Sydney didn't have to worry about getting her clothes messy or disturbing her perfect hairstyle. She could just be Sydney, and that was all she'd ever asked for.

Chapter Five

Sydney wasn't even a little bit surprised to see Lewis walk into Alice's house with Albert that evening. Alice grinned at her brother-in-law. "Oh, good! I was hoping I could rope you into having supper with us!"

"I'm surprised Susan let you steal her guest for the evening," Lewis said, grinning at Sydney.

"Me too," Alice said. "I think she was hoping her ultimate plans will be better served with a small group of people at supper."

Sydney rolled her eyes. "Just say it. She wants Lewis and I to marry and give her a dozen grandchildren."

"Make that two dozen, and you'll be right," Lewis said, winking at her. "She loves the idea of having children she can spoil and then send home to their parents."

"She's very good at doing just that!" Alice said, looking down at little Rachel, who was playing on the floor with an old rag doll.

"I'm almost afraid to even think about that," Sydney said, shaking her head. "I feel like people are trying to plan my life for me, just like they did back in Beckham."

Alice stopped what she was doing and looked at her new friend. "Not at all. It's all good natured. If you meet a man at church you prefer, no one would be even the least bit upset. You are free to marry whomever you wish here."

"I do hope you wish to marry me, though," Lewis said.

"I've had a meal with you, taken a walk with you, and shared one kiss. I have a feeling I should know you a little better than that before I agree to marry you."

"Another kiss or two might convince her," Albert said, slapping his brother on the shoulder.

"Maybe if she saw my house..." Lewis said.

Albert shook his head. "Looks just like mine. And now I've saved your reputation from ruin, and you don't have to be alone in Lewis's house with him."

Sydney laughed. "I think it's silly for reputations to be ruined so easily. My mother had maids following me for a long time, but then when I started riding my bicycle, they couldn't keep up."

"I want to take a turn on that contraption of yours," Lewis said, smiling at her. "Would you mind teaching me to ride?"

"I'd love to! I can't teach Susan or Alice since they're both expecting, but I can teach any of you menfolk."

Lewis and Albert exchanged a glance. "Susan is expecting again?" Albert asked.

"Oh, was that supposed to be a secret?" Sydney felt terrible breaking the news to Susan's stepsons that way. She was certain the other woman would prefer to tell people herself.

Alice shrugged. "She didn't tell us it was a secret, so you can't be upset with yourself for saying something."

Sydney sighed. "I guess I can't, but it still feels as though I've done something wrong."

"You haven't." Alice put the food on the table before picking up Rachel and putting her in her highchair.

Once the four adults were sitting, they bowed their heads automatically, and Lewis said a prayer over the meal.

"I love your chicken and dumplings even more than Susan's," Lewis said, looking excited about the meal.

"It looks and smells delicious," Sydney said, looking forward to trying the new meal.

"Wait until you taste it!" Albert said excitedly. "I could eat this every night for a month."

"A beef rancher loving chicken that much? Isn't that against the law?" Lewis asked his brother.

"Shhhsh," Albert said.

Lewis laughed as he took his first bite of the dumplings, looking ecstatic. "Best batch I've had the pleasure of eating, Alice. Are you sure you don't want to get rid of this awful husband of yours and marry me? I'd let you cook this every night!"

Alice just smiled, watching Sydney to see her reaction.

Sydney cut off a little piece of a dumpling with her spoon, and got some gravy and a bit of chicken, wanting to try all the flavors at once. She took one bite and smiled happily. "This is wonderful! I've missed out on so much with my mother hating chicken."

"Don't worry. You'll have all those experiences here with us," Lewis said with a grin. Well, unless she married someone else. He found he was already feeling bereft at the thought. He needed to get her to agree to marry him before they went to church on Sunday, and she met all the cowboys who would wander in for the service.

"There's a church social on Saturday night," Albert pointed out, nudging his brother.

"Would you care to go to the church social with me?" Lewis asked.

Sydney nodded, a smile transforming her face from merely pretty to absolutely beautiful. "I would love to. I've never been to a church social." She didn't know what was supposed to happen at a church social, but she'd wear a pretty dress and enjoy herself no matter what happened.

Alice frowned. "Your mother was dragging you everywhere to find you a husband, and she never took you to a church social? That's how I met all the young men in the area."

"My mother didn't want me to marry just anyone. She was looking for a rich man who came from old wealth." Sydney rolled her eyes. "One of those boring men who talks about nothing but himself."

Alice shook her head. "Your mother sounds like an odd one. I don't remember speaking to her often, but I certainly remember how she was with you."

"My mother didn't speak to people working in simple shops like the mercantile. She was more interested in speaking to people in modiste shops. The most important thing in her world is making certain that I wore a gown that fitted me perfectly. If it didn't make my waist look tiny, then it wasn't good enough."

"I'm glad you're here," Alice said softly. "And you really must marry before your parents discover where you are."

Sydney nodded. "I know. I would rather wait for some time to get to know someone well, but I probably only have a week before I need to just marry anyone."

Lewis frowned. "Are you saying I'm just anyone?" He felt as if she was not at all interested in him as he was in her. She wasn't just a marriage prospect to him. She was the woman he felt he'd waited his whole life for.

"Not at all," Sydney said. "I'm sorry if that sounded rude. I just hate that I must be in a rush. I'd rather make you court me for a few years before we marry."

"And I'd rather be married to you tomorrow."

"I'm not sure that's the best idea," Sydney said. "Let's at least give it til Sunday. Then we can enjoy the church social, and I can recover from my journey here before we do anything else."

"All right," Lewis said. "Today's just Tuesday, so five days from now? I can wait that long for an answer, as long as you let me get to know you in the meantime."

"Of course, I will," Sydney said. "Don't worry, you are first on my list."

"There's a list?" Alice asked.

Sydney shook her head. "You're all just trying to trap me into saying something I don't mean."

Albert grinned at her. "I suppose you already know us."

After supper was finished, Lewis invited Sydney to go for a walk. "Let me help with the dishes first," Sydney replied.

Alice shook her head. "No, you're our guest. I'll do the dishes." She made a shooing motion with her hand.

"I'm perfectly capable of helping!" Sydney said. Why had she learned all the skills she had at the orphanage if not to actually use them?

"You'll be doing dishes as soon as you're married. Let us spoil you for a little while."

"But I've been spoiled all my life!"

Alice just laughed and turned away.

Sydney followed Lewis outside, and they walked in a different direction than they had the night before. After walking a short way, he pointed straight ahead. "That's my house. It really is exactly the same as Albert's."

"Looks nice," she said. Sydney wasn't certain about being the wife of a horse breeder, but she really liked Lewis. What she knew of him anyway. "So, tell me what a typical day is like for you."

"Well, I'm not much for cooking, so I start my day by going to my Pa and Susan's house. I eat breakfast with that crazy group. And then I go through the stable, checking each of the horses for any injuries or anything wrong with them. I check the mares' cycles regularly, because I need to know when I should plan to breed them."

"Wait," she said, stopping walking. "You actually put them together so they can...make a baby?"

He grinned. "How else do you think we breed them?"

"I don't know! I guess I was picturing a little marriage ceremony where the mare wears a white veil and the stallion a tie. Then you make them a bed of roses in the stable, and hang curtains so they have their privacy..."

He laughed. "Well, you certainly have an imagination. Perhaps you should write children's books about animals."

"Perhaps I will," she said grinning at him.

He led her into the stables and showed her their prize stallion. "I'm still trying to find the perfect mare for him. We've bred him multiple times, and his foals always end up being the best ones we have. Of course, if we had the perfect mare for him, we'd have prize foals year after year. It would really help us out with the breeding and training business."

Sydney took a step closer to the stall the stallion was in, stroking his nose with one hand. "What's his name?" she asked.

"Renegade."

"Hello, Renegade." She blew out a breath in the horse's face, so he could get to know her scent.

Lewis was surprised. "Have you been around horses a lot?"

Sydney grinned. "I've always liked horses, and I ran down to the stable every minute I had to see them what I was a little girl. My mother didn't think a girl of my station should be spending much time with horses though, so I had to sneak away. She was more riled up when I rode my bicycle anyway."

Lewis grinned. "And you wanted her riled up?"

"It was the only time she showed any real emotion. When she was yelling at me. She wanted a boy, you see..."

"I'm sorry. Does it help if I tell you that I like you just the way you are?" he asked, catching her hand, and pulling her to him for a stolen kiss.

"I think I like you just how you are as well. Oh, Lewis, are we doing the right thing? We just met yesterday, and I feel like we're halfway to an engagement already."

"I don't know if it's the right thing for you, but you're certainly not my first opportunity to marry. I've met a lot of girls over the years, but you're the one who interests me the most. I...I already feel like I'm half in love with you, and you act as if I'm the first man you saw when you got into town, so you feel obligated to think about marrying me."

"That's not how I feel at all! I just...I've never met any man that I could marry that I had any desire to marry. I just met all the terrible men my mother paraded me in front of, and then I met men that I wasn't allowed to marry. It's just a different feeling, and I'm afraid I'm jumping into things too quickly, though I don't have a choice. I know that probably didn't explain things at all."

"It did. I understand. But I do hope you'll choose me. To make things a bit easier..." He dropped to one knee right there in the stable. "Will you marry me?" At the look of shock on her face, he said, "You don't have to tell me now. If you'll give me an answer on Sunday, I will be very pleased."

Sydney took a deep breath. "You'll have your answer on Sunday. Thank you for allowing me a few days to just be Sydney and not my mother's daughter and not Mrs. Dailey. I need to be me for a little while if that makes sense?"

"It does. I've never been in a position where I couldn't be me. I've always known that whoever I chose to be on a certain day would be just fine with my family. I think in your position, I might just feel the same as you do."

"Thank you for trying to understand me," Sydney said, waiting until Lewis got back on his feet and throwing her arms around him. "You are the only man I've ever met that I have a desire to consider marrying, if that's at all helpful."

He chuckled. "You just keep making me feel better and better." But he did understand. Whether he wanted to or not, he needed to know that she was going to be happy with whatever decision she made.

He walked her back toward the main house on the ranch, where she was staying with Susan's family. "How long have you had your own house?" she asked as they walked along.

"A few years," he said, twining his fingers through hers. "Albert and I built them at the same time. We'd build one bedroom, and then we'd go to the other house and build the exact same bedroom. I love my little house. And I'd make sure it was clean before we ever married."

She laughed. "I enjoy cleaning, but that's probably because I've never had to do it on a regular basis. I look forward to cleaning up after you and cooking your meals."

"You do? Does that mean you're leaning toward accepting my proposal?"

"It does. You know I am."

When they reached the house, he pulled her into his arms and kissed her goodnight. "Dream of me and the life we'll have together once you stop being stubborn," he said.

"Stubborn?"

Before she could get riled up, he dropped a kiss on her nose. "I'll see you tomorrow."

She smiled. "Why does tomorrow sound like a promise all of a sudden and not like something I should dread?"

"Because your mother is no longer ruling your every action. I just hope we're already married before she sends someone after you."

"I'm sure my papa will give me a head start and say he found the note later than he actually did. He never liked how mother would try to force things I didn't want on me."

"I hope you're right. I don't know if I could let you go back to Massachusetts." He kissed her once more and then opened his father's front door for her. "Goodnight, Sydney. I'll see you in the evening."

Sydney smiled, wondering if Susan would allow her to take over her kitchen. It might be nice to fix a meal for him all on her own, and they could eat it together, outside somewhere. It was certainly warm enough. That's one thing she could say for the Texas weather. It was warmer than it would have been in Beckham, and they could start having summer-type fun.

Chapter Six

Shortly after waking up the following day—after noon again to Sydney's dismay—she met up with Susan and asked permission to make a picnic supper for herself and Lewis in the kitchen.

Susan nodded. "Of course. Hopefully you'll find something you want to cook."

"Well, I was thinking of just making peanut butter and jelly sandwiches."

"What's peanut butter?"

"Oh, Susan, you haven't had the privilege of eating peanut butter yet? Where's the nearest store? I'll go and buy some and bring enough for everyone. My bicycle is still right outside."

Susan frowned at her. "I really don't think you should ride your bicycle miles in this heat. Why don't I have one of the twins take you instead? Thomas is always looking for ways to go into town so he can try to catch a glimpse of what's happening in Hell's Half Acre. I think I'll send you with Walter."

Sydney started to protest, but the truth was, she wasn't looking forward to the ride anyway. It had to be five miles, and it was just so hot! "I'd like that if it's no trouble."

"None at all. I have some grape jelly I put up last year. Will that work for the jelly part of the sandwiches? We'll bake some bread as soon as you get back."

"Sounds wonderful. Thank you, Susan! I can't believe how kind you've been to a total stranger who showed up at your doorstep."

"Oh, that reminds me! I got a reply to my telegram from Elizabeth, thanking me for helping you out, and letting me know she won't send anyone else to marry Randy Ranch. I still can't believe that happened to you." Susan looked around. "We should make some potato salad to go with the sandwiches. I haven't made that in forever, and since it's Mrs. Hackenschleimer's day off, today is a good day. I'll serve the family whatever we make for your picnic."

Sydney smiled. "Oh, good. Then I can help with the family meal."

"Yes, I'll allow it just this once. We should make a couple of pies as well. Why not? It's going to be a glorious day!"

"I like pie!" Sydney said. "I've never made it though because the orphans didn't have dessert often. Not so much because there was no money for dessert but because there was no money for dentists."

"Well, I'll teach you. I canned some pie filling last fall. We could do apple, pumpkin, or cherry? Do you have a preference?" Susan looked excited to cook with her, and Sydney couldn't be happier.

"Should I run and ask David if I can steal Walter to take me to town?" Sydney knew she should probably just start riding, but she had no desire to go that far on her bicycle. Not in the heat of the day. And it was only spring! Surely, she'd melt into a little puddle by the middle of the summer.

"Yes, tell David I said he has to be the one to go." Susan shook her head. "Thomas is starting to worry me more than a little bit."

"I'm sure he'll turn out fine, just as his older brothers did."

"I pray you're right."

Sydney hurried out to the corral outside the stable, finding David, Thomas, and Walter all working there. "Lewis is in the stable!" David called out to her.

Sydney opened her mouth to shout back, but she decided that wouldn't be exactly ladylike, and she was trying to at least pretend she was a lady—well, if you ignored the bloomers and bicycle.

Instead, Sydney walked to David and told him Susan had told her to have Walter drive her into town. "I want to go!" one of the twins said, and she could only assume that one was Thomas. They did look identical.

"Your mother said Walter, so Walter is the one going."

Thomas kicked a clump of dirt. "I never get to go anywhere."

"You're going to the church social on Saturday night, aren't you?" Sydney asked.

"Yes, but I want to go to the Acre."

"And that's why Walter is driving her," David said, shaking his head at his son. "Have you forgotten your Uncle Jesse died in the Acre?"

"No, but...I just want to see what happens there, and why I'm forbidden from going."

David looked at his son for a moment. "Men drink, gamble, and purchase a few minutes with a whore there. Now you know."

Walter had hurried away to hitch up the wagon while they were talking, so instead of stand there and argue with Thomas, Sydney hurried off in the direction of the carriage house. It seemed odd to her they needed a carriage house, but when she walked inside, she understood. There were four buggies inside, including two of what her mother would have called, 'those dreadful courting buggies.'

Walter was working on hitching up a simple wagon. "I assume we're shopping, so I'm taking the wagon with the most storage."

"Well, I thank you for that. We are getting a few things, so the extra space will be nice." Sydney had a mind to shop for some new fabric in town. She had her old clothes that she'd worn when she volunteered at the orphanage and she had her nice clothes. There was nothing for her to wear as a new wife. She did have a wedding gown already made, but that was because her mother wanted her married off before she could complain.

Walter handed her up into the wagon before sliding the doors out of the way, so they could head out. "What are we shopping for?"

"Well, initially I was just going to get peanut butter, but I think I'm going to buy some calico for a couple of dresses as well."

"If you plan to marry Lewis, you may want fabric for curtains and a tablecloth and nice things ladies want around." Walter watched straight ahead, obviously comfortable driving to town. "What's peanut butter?"

"Oh, it's this wonderful thing you spread on bread for sandwiches. I've been known to even eat it with a spoon."

"I may need to try some of that," he said.

"I hope you don't mind sitting for a few minutes while I shop," she said.

"'Course not. This is your errand not mine. I'm happy enough getting away from work for a few hours."

Sydney smiled. "At least you're honest."

"Always!" Walter grinned as he continued driving, turning on a street into town.

He pulled over in front of a store in a part of town she hadn't been in yet, and she hoped that meant she was far from Hell's Half Acre.

Before he could offer to help her down, she'd jumped and hurried inside the door. She quickly walked around until she found the most important thing she'd come for, the peanut butter. She purchased six jars, simply because she was certain Susan was going to love it as much as she did.

And then she walked to the fabrics to do the fun part of her shopping. She chose a soft green flower pattern for her first dress, and a plain yellow for the second. For her third and fourth dresses, she bought white with lavender polka dots, and then a plain pink.

Then she looked at fabric for curtains and a tablecloth. She tended to favor different shades of purple, so she bought fifteen yards of a lilac. Taking all to the front of the store, she paid with some of the cash she had in her reticule and was happy when a young man offered to carry her purchases out to her wagon.

The young man and Walter chatted while they loaded the wagon, and Sydney sat waiting patiently on the wagon seat.

It was less than an hour and a half since she'd left the house when Walter stopped the wagon in front of it. "Thank you so much for driving me, Walter."

"Happy to do it. I'll get everything inside, if you want to go and have some of the lemonade, I'm sure Ma made while we were out. She thinks we're all going to die of the heat when we leave, and her lemonade is the only thing that will save us."

Sydney laughed softly. "Thank you again, and I think I will take you up on some of your mother's lemonade." She went into the house and went straight to the kitchen and the ice box that was sitting in the corner. It was the largest ice box she'd ever seen, and when she looked, she realized there were three. Well, that made sense with the amount of people who ate in that house.

She found the pitcher, just as Susan walked into the kitchen. "Did you get the peanut butter?" Susan asked.

"I did. I got a lot. And I got some fabric for some everyday dresses and some for making curtains and pillows and tablecloths. I'm excited to make them all. Mother never let me sew, but I learned how at the orphanage."

"You've made a dress though?" Susan asked.

"I have. Several in fact."

"Have you used a sewing machine? I have one in the parlor, and I find it to be one of the best purchases we ever made. You'll learn to use it quickly, even if you've never touched one."

Sydney's eyes widened. "I haven't used one! Mrs. Anderson at the orphanage was always talking about how it would be such a joy to use one and save her fingers, but she never did get one."

"That's sad. If I sent her the money for a sewing machine, and told her that's what it was for, would she buy the machine, or simply use it for food for the children?"

"She'd buy the machine. The orphans grow a great deal of the food they need in their own garden, and there are cows to milk, and eggs are there in the henhouse. They buy little food. And the sewing machine would be used daily for sewing, mending, and maybe even for stitching the kids up after they've fallen out of trees onto each other." Sydney could just picture Mrs. Anderson's face if she received a donation for a sewing machine. "I tried to get my mother to buy her a machine, and she told me that with as much time as I spent at the orphanage, they could buy the machine from the labor costs they'd saved."

Susan frowned. "Knowing that, I'll send money for a machine, and for the cost of fabric for several dresses."

Sydney clapped her hands and hugged Susan. "I'm so glad I found you. Just think where I could be if I hadn't, and now you're helping my orphans as well? I couldn't ask for a better friend."

Walter brought the jars into the kitchen. "Do you want me to put the fabric in the parlor, Ma?"

"Yes, please." Susan looked at Sydney. "Now let's bake some bread for these sandwiches."

Together the two women baked eight loaves of bread. When Sydney tried to protest it was too many, Susan shook her head. "If the men like these sandwiches of yours we'll use more than half that on supper tonight."

"I can understand that," Sydney said, though she still had her doubts.

Once the bread was in the oven, Susan showed Sydney how to make a pie crust. "I'll give you the receipt and all my others when you marry."

"That would be wonderful."

"I've already started copying them for you. Since you are coming from a family of wealth, there's no real question as to whether you'll need them."

Sydney nodded eagerly. "I need all the help I can get." She frowned. "Oh, snotdragons. I forgot to buy fabric for aprons and nightdresses. I always wear these silk nightgowns because that's all my mother would allow. They are much too hot here, in my opinion."

"I have plenty of muslin for aprons and nightdresses. Don't worry about that."

"I'll make certain to replace it."

"No need. It's part of my wedding gift to you."

Sydney made a face. "You realize I'm still not certain if it's Lewis I want to marry?"

"Of course, I do. I'm not even trying to push you in his direction. You choose who you want to be married to, and I'll be happy for you."

Susan took the bread from the oven and slipped the pies inside. "Now let's make our potato salad."

"I have no idea how."

"You will soon. You'll get the receipt for this as well."

Together they boiled potatoes and eggs, sliced them, and turned them into the most delicious potato salad Sydney had ever seen. Of course, that hadn't taken much. Her mother had said potato salad was for poor people, and she'd never even had one taste.

Sydney stared at it for a moment, and then she asked, "May I try a bite? I've never had potato salad."

"I don't know how you stayed alive!" Susan said, reaching for a clean spoon, and handing it to Sydney.

Sydney dipped the spoon into the potato salad before putting it in her mouth, a smile transforming her face. "It's delicious."

"It is. And you'll serve it to Lewis. Do you have any idea where you'll go on your picnic?"

Sydney nodded. "I've been eyeing your gazebo since I got here. I thought that would be a nice romantic spot for a picnic, and a little talking." *And some kissing. There'd better be some kissing.*

As soon as the bread cooled, Sydney introduced Susan to a peanut butter and jelly sandwich. Carefully slathering peanut butter on one piece of bread, she added some grape jelly to the other piece. And then she smooshed them together and cut the sandwich down the middle, offering half to Susan.

Susan took a bite and her eyes widened. "This is good!"

"Yes, even small children like it. I haven't found anyone yet who isn't fond of peanut butter." Sydney bit into her own half, realizing just then she'd yet to eat that day. It was odd to feel too busy to eat, but that's just how she'd felt all day. She couldn't wait to start cutting on her new dresses.

Susan swallowed the last of her part of the sandwich. "Why don't we invite some friends of mine over tomorrow. And Alice, of course. We'll have a tea party sewing what you need."

Sydney's eyes grew wide. "No one would mind helping me that way?" The only time anyone had ever helped Sydney had been when they were paid to do so. She truly felt as if she'd fallen out of her world into one where people worked together to get things done, and where they helped one another, even if they didn't expect anything in return.

In short, she'd fallen into a very hot version of heaven.

Chapter Seven

Just before it was time for the men to arrive for supper, Sydney started doubting herself. What if no one liked the peanut butter and jelly? It had been such a simple thing to make for the orphans, and they'd all seemed to love it, but none of the Daileys had ever eaten peanut butter! Hopefully she hadn't steered Susan wrong, and everyone would enjoy the meal.

Sydney had packed the picnic into a picnic basket Susan had offered her for the evening. It made her feel as if it was a real picnic, and not as it was when she just let the orphans eat outside in their own yard. She couldn't wait to eat in the gazebo. It just seemed to be made for picnics. Every time she looked at it, all she could think about was having a picnic there.

But she was sure Lewis had already had dozens of picnics there. What if he didn't like her choice of locale? What if he hated peanut butter? She had no idea if she should follow through with her plans or figure something else out.

"Stop fretting," Susan said, shaking her head. "He's going to love the food. He's going to enjoy anything the two of you do together. So just go and have fun."

"I can do that," Sydney said, straightening her spine. "I'm a calm, confident woman."

When Lewis came in with his brothers and father, he had an odd look on his face, and he looked through the room until he saw Sydney standing apart from the others, looking as beautiful as she always did. He seemed relieved to see her, and Sydney wasn't sure what was going on in his head.

"I have our picnic ready," she said to him. "I thought we could eat it in the gazebo."

He nodded, looking a tad bit worried. "That will be fine."

"Is something happening that I don't know about?" she asked.

"We'll talk while we eat." He opened the front door for her, and she followed, carrying the picnic basket.

She was surprised he seemed so distracted, and he hadn't even offered to carry the basket. That was unlike Lewis, at least unlike what she knew of him so far. "Something is wrong," Sydney said, looking around. What could have happened between their farewell kiss the night before and this afternoon?

Lewis nodded, only then reaching for the basket. "Do you know how to shoot?" he asked.

"Shoot?" What kind of a question was that? "Of course, I don't know how to shoot. Should I?"

"It would be good if you did." He frowned at her. "Someone was looking for you today. By name. They said they'd been hired to return you to Beckham."

"What? How are they here so quickly?"

"I have no idea. Aunt Elizabeth wouldn't have told anyone you were here if she knew you didn't want people to know."

She sighed. "They've found me already." It felt as if her careful plans were crashing down around her in ruins.

"No, they were checking all the ranches in the area. They don't know you're here. But they will soon." He shook his head. "As far as I know, they may be checking all the western towns. I just think decisions should be made quickly."

She shook her head. "Well, I suppose we should marry...tonight if we can."

"I thought you wanted more time?"

"I *would* like more time. I don't always get what I want. I learned that at a young age." Sydney couldn't believe their picnic had already been ruined. "I just wanted to have one picnic."

He shook his head. "Let's have your picnic. We'll talk to Susan and Pa after supper to see if we can make it happen tonight, or first thing tomorrow." He put his hand over hers. "I'm delighted to marry you, but I didn't want it to happen this way. I wanted you to be able to have your days of freedom and make your choice."

"And now there's no way for that to happen. I understand."

As they ate, she explained all she and Susan had done that afternoon to get the food ready, amusing him with her trip into town to buy peanut butter. "You were going to ride your bicycle all the way to Fort Worth?" he asked.

"I rode it all the way out here on the day I arrived," she said, grinning at him, even as her eyes scanned everything around them, waiting for someone to jump out of the bushes at her.

"Well, you weren't being searched for then. Not around here at any rate."

"I'm sure it was smart for Walter to drive me into town, but I do enjoy riding my bicycle, and I won't ever stop." Her words were a warning to him. He wasn't going to get her bicycle away from her.

"How long have you been riding your bicycle?"

She smiled at that. "When I was twelve, I was pudgy, and my mother was looking for a way to get me to exercise more, so she bought me a bicycle. She told my father they'd let me ride it for a few months, and then they'd give it to the orphanage. Well, I loved it so much, my father refused to let her give it away. He told her it was my favorite thing, and no matter how she wanted me to live, I was keeping my bicycle."

"I'm not noticing even an ounce of extra weight on you," he said, his eyes traveling up and down her body. "I like everything just the way it is."

She grinned, shaking her head at him. "You're not supposed to look at me like that!"

"Why not?" he asked. "We're getting married tomorrow at the latest, right?"

Sydney nodded. "We are."

"So, I'm going to look at you as if you're my wife, because that's what you are."

She laughed. "I think you're jumping the gun a little, but I guess I don't mind too much."

"Maybe I am. I'm just happy it's going to finally happen!"

"Finally?" she asked. "I met you two days ago!"

"It seems like so much longer."

"I don't know why it feels different than getting off the train and immediately marrying a stranger, but it does."

Lewis nodded. "I understand." He finished the piece of pie she'd included for him. "I think we should get back inside. I'm sorry we can't linger over our picnic."

"We probably shouldn't have eaten outside at all. I hope those men don't find me."

He stood up and gathered the remains from their picnic, and then held his hand down to help her up.

Sydney smiled up at him and reached up to take his hand. "I guess I'll be taking your hand a lot in the future."

"I guess you will."

She still wasn't sure marrying him was the right thing to do, but not marrying him wasn't an option. Unless she wanted to marry Thomas or Walter, and they didn't seem older than seventeen. It might be old enough to some people, but it wasn't to her. `-

Walking back into the house, Lewis nodded at his father. "We want to get married tonight if we can."

Susan looked surprised. "Did something happen?"

"I'll fill you in later," David said.

Thomas jumped up. "Want me to go get the preacher?"

Susan shook her head. "I want Walter to go get the preacher. I don't trust you wandering around on your own right now."

"But Ma! I never actually went into the Acre!"

"You were seen heading toward it. That's enough for me."

Thomas scowled but didn't argue more. Walter got up and went out to get the wagon.

It was then that Sydney realized they were all still eating. "I'm sorry to interrupt your supper!" she said.

Susan shook her head. "We were just finishing up." She looked curious about why the plans had changed so quickly, but she didn't ask again. "Do you have a dress you want to wear for the wedding?"

Sydney nodded. "My mother paid a ridiculous amount of money for my wedding dress. I may as well wear it." She started up the stairs to her room and the trunk of her belongings that had arrived with Susan right behind her.

"I'll help however I can."

"I know you will."

"Tell me why we're in a hurry?"

Sydney grinned. She wasn't certain she could have waited to find out what was happening either. "Men came here today looking for me."

"You think your parents sent them?"

"I'm sure of it. So, I need to be married. If I'm married, then they can't force me to go back to Beckham." Sydney dug through her trunk, finding her wedding dress, which had been carefully wrapped with tissue paper so it wouldn't wrinkle. "Besides, my mother won't want me back if I'm married. No one will want to marry someone who's been married before. Well, no one she wants me to marry."

Susan shook her head. "I'm so glad you got away from her!" She gasped as Sydney pulled the gown from the trunk and held it in front of her. "That is the most beautiful wedding dress I have ever seen. I've noticed the trend has been white dresses lately. Did you want a white wedding dress?"

"What I want just didn't seem to matter. Queen Victoria was married in white, and so I will be married in white."

"Well, I guess that settles it. Let's get you dressed."

Thirty minutes later, Sydney stood in her wedding gown gazing into the mirror in her small room. Susan had fixed her hair atop her head, and she felt like she was about to be paraded in front of many men at a ball.

"I hate looking like this," Sydney said.

"Do you want me to change something?" Susan asked. "You look beautiful."

Sydney frowned. "No, don't change anything. This is how my mother always wanted me to look. I wanted to wear my bloomers."

Susan laughed. "You really can wear your bloomers here, just probably not to church."

Sydney's response was laughter. "Oh, even I wouldn't dare wear bloomers to church!"

A knock on the door revealed one of Susan's older daughters. "The preacher is here."

Susan took Sydney by the shoulders. "You're going to be so happy with Lewis. I promise!"

"I just hope he's happy with me." Sydney wasn't certain she had the right skills to be a housewife. She'd learn though.

Susan went ahead of her, and she slowly walked down the stairs, careful to not step on the long train of the dress. She hadn't wanted a train, but her mother had insisted. As usual.

When she got to the parlor where the family had gathered for their small wedding, she grinned at Alice, who was there with everyone else. Someone must have gone to fetch her, which thrilled Sydney. She hadn't thought of it until that moment, but she did want her friend there with her.

Stopping at Lewis's side, she smiled up at him. He was a good man, and she was going to be the best wife she knew how to be.

The ceremony was short and simple. When the preacher said, "You may kiss the bride," Sydney was a bit stunned it was over so quickly. She raised her lips for Lewis's kiss and giggled when he bent her back over his arm with their first kiss as a married couple.

There were cheers from the family, and she turned and locked her eyes with Susan's. "Thank you!"

"I just wished we'd made a big cake today instead of pie," Susan said, sighing. "Pastor, would you like some pie before Walter takes you home?"

"I wondered which twin it was who came for me. Thank you, Walter," the pastor said, looking at Walter. "Now I know who came for me, I can tell you apart by your shirts. It's harder when you dress the same for church on Sundays." Then he looked over at Susan. "I think I'd enjoy a piece of pie. My wife is visiting her mother this month, and as much as I enjoy eating what the ladies in church bring to me, I do miss my wife's pies."

Sydney wondered if some day, she would be away from Lewis, and he would miss something she cooked for him. She hoped so, but she thought not. Her cooking skills would have to improve dramatically before then. She had a feeling Lewis wouldn't like peanut butter and jelly too often, and it was one of the few meals she knew how to make.

Following everyone back into the dining room, they ate the third and fourth pies she and Susan had made that day. There was an apple and a cherry, and though she preferred cherry, Sydney chose the apple. She didn't want to get cherry all over her wedding dress. No, she'd pack that right back into her trunk so her daughter could wear it someday. But only if she wanted to.

After the pie and coffee, Walter left to take the pastor home. Albert and Thomas were tasked with carrying Sydney's trunk to Lewis's house. After they'd gone, Lewis looked at Sydney. "Are you ready to go?"

"I should change into another dress. I don't want to get grass stains on my wedding dress."

He frowned at her. "Why? You planning on wearing it again?"

She laughed. "No, I was hoping our daughter would wear it someday."

"I like that idea. You look absolutely beautiful tonight. Have I told you that yet?"

Sydney shook her head. "I hope you see more than just my face."

"You know I do!" Lewis said, but she wondered. How could she not? They'd known one another for precisely two days, and how could a marriage last when they were strangers?

"I'll change and be right back down," she said.

He watched her as she climbed the stairs, thinking about how truly beautiful she was. And kind. And loving. And free-spirited. She was a bloomers-wearing, bicycle-riding lady from the east. And he was going to hold on to her as tightly as he could.

David walked up behind him and clapped him on the back. "Do I need to give you the good husband talk?"

"No. I sat in on the one you had with Albert. I'll be just fine."

"Just treat her as you would like to see your sisters treated."

Those words struck Lewis. He had several sisters, and he couldn't imagine a man treating any of them poorly. He would hurt any man who so much as looked at one of his sisters wrong. And then he understood what his father was saying. He should treat Sydney exactly how he thought his sisters should be treated by their future husbands.

As if they were made of spun glass.

Chapter Eight

As soon as Sydney had changed into the dress she'd worn earlier, she hurried down the stairs, stopping at the bottom to ask Susan, "Are we still going to do that little sewing party tomorrow?"

"We are. I've invited several friends, and they've said they'll come."

"What do I need to bring?"

Susan shook her head. "Fabric. That's all. And I have some for nightgowns and aprons, so you don't need to worry about those."

"Thank you!"

"Welcome to the family, Sydney!"

"Do I call you Ma now? Or can I keep calling you Susan?"

Susan laughed softly. "Lewis doesn't call me Ma, so I don't know why you would think you needed to."

"I guess I feel like it's showing respect for you."

"Show your respect by being my friend."

Sydney grinned. "Of all the potential mothers-in-law I was forced to socialize with, you're my very favorite."

"I'd better be," Susan said. "And you can be my favorite daughter-in-law every other day. Well, until some of the others marry, of course."

"Of course." Sydney hugged her friend and then hurried over to Lewis. "I have my carpet bag. I'll get the wedding dress from Susan tomorrow. I'm coming over for a sewing party."

Lewis nodded. "I don't understand how you can have a party and work at the same time, but I'm not going to say anything. How can I?"

Sydney shrugged. "No idea. Probably best if you stay quiet," she said, grinning up at him. "Let's go home."

As they walked toward the house, Lewis brought up a subject she hadn't been able to discuss with him yet. "If you want to delay the wedding night, we can do that," he said softly.

Sydney loved the idea, and it took everything inside her not to say that's what she wanted, but she knew procrastinating wouldn't make their first time any easier. Nothing would except just doing it. "No, this is our wedding night." Besides, she knew if she was no longer a virgin, her mother would have to leave her alone.

"Well, you just made me the happiest man on earth," Lewis said, grinning at her.

She grinned at him. "Happy to have done so. And thank you for being willing to just handle the wedding immediately. It wasn't the most romantic way we could have gotten married, but it was a necessity."

He led her to his front door and then frowned. "Before Alice came, Susan and Mrs. Hackenschleimer cleaned Albert's house. I didn't have a chance to have anyone do that for you!"

"That's all right. Being a wife means that I cook and clean and I do it all with a smile on my face, right?"

"I'm not so sure about the smile part..."

He opened the door, and she peered inside, expecting a mess, but instead, she saw two of his sisters there, with a bucket. "We just finished," Augusta, the oldest of the Dailey girls, said.

"Thank you!" Sydney said, hugging each of the girls in turn. "You have no idea how wonderful this wedding gift of yours was."

The girls smiled happily as they hurried off to their home.

Lewis looked around, surprised at how clean the house was. "How did they do that so fast?"

"They've been taught to clean house and cook from the time they learned to walk. Of course, they can do it quickly and efficiently."

"They complain when Susan asks them to clean. They looked happy here!"

"When you have to do it at home, it's called chores. When you can do it for your brand-new sister-in-law as a surprise, you feel much better about yourself." Sydney understood perfectly, though she'd never been in the girls' situation. Not exactly. "Wait, do you have a bathroom? I know Albert does."

"I do," Lewis said proudly, walking her to the bathroom and showing her. "Susan said it was the best thing that could have been waiting for her when she married. So, she insisted we put them into our homes for our future wives."

"I need to thank her again. How many times can I thank her? I cannot believe all she's done to make my life easier."

Sydney hurried to the kitchen and looked inside the ice box, praying he had something she would know how to cook. There were eggs in a bowl on the counter, and there was a small bit of bacon. There was no other food she could see. "What do you usually eat?" she asked.

"Whatever Mrs. Hackenschleimer cooks. I don't have any idea how long those eggs have been there, and I think the bacon in the ice box could walk away on its own." Lewis shrugged. "It was easier eating at my parents' house."

"Do you consider Susan your mother?" she asked.

He frowned at the question. "I was six when my mother died. I have vague memories of her, but Susan is responsible for making me who I am. She is the one who drilled manners into our heads and who taught us right from wrong. I do think of her as my mother, but I just never started calling her Ma. It was different for the twins. Our mother died when they were born, and Susan is the only mother they've ever known. But Albert and I...we should have called her Ma. I don't know why we didn't."

Sydney nodded. His round-about answer told her what she needed to know. He considered Susan his mother, just didn't call her that. Easy enough. "I want to look at everything. Is that all right?"

"Of course. There are two bedrooms up and one down. We have the downstairs room. It's big enough for a cradle in the corner so that we can keep the babies in our room until they are big enough to be upstairs on their own."

"That's a good plan. I really love the idea of having several children. Don't you?"

"Definitely. If my family isn't bigger than my pa's, I'll feel like I've failed as a man."

Sydney's jaw dropped. "You want more than eleven children? I was thinking four or five." She'd joked about having a dozen or two, but she hadn't meant it!

Lewis grinned. "Why don't we just wait and see how many God blesses us with?"

"That's a great idea," she told him, still a little wary of the idea of so many. Though Susan was expecting child number eleven, and she didn't seem even a little upset about it.

Lewis waited as she ran up the stairs and looked at the bedrooms there, and then she explored the entire first floor. The kitchen, the parlor, the bathroom, and the bedroom, as well as a large pantry off the kitchen.

"Cellar?" she asked. At that point she didn't know if she was exploring because she was curious or because she was trying to put off their wedding night, but it didn't matter. She had to see every inch of the house, and it had to happen right then.

He went into the pantry and lifted the cellar door for her. "You're not going to be able to see down there." It was already getting dark, and he could barely see upstairs. "Let me get you a lantern."

He hurried and got the lantern, and then he lit a second one for the upstairs. "There you go." Instead of following her down, he waited upstairs.

"There's no food down there!" she exclaimed.

"I'm aware. We're going to have to go into town for provisions, but perhaps you could just give me a list, and we can send Walter. I'm not leaving your side, but I'm also not taking you into town with those men looking out for you."

"But you'll leave me at your mother's house for the sewing party, right?"

He frowned. "As long as Alice has her gun, I suppose that will be all right."

"Why would Alice having her gun have anything to do with it?" Sydney asked.

He grinned. "Alice is a crack shot. She had to shoot the same man twice when she first got here, and she hit him just exactly where she was aiming. She's a better shot than Albert, who is the best shot of us boys."

"She told me she could teach me to shoot, but I didn't think she was really serious."

"Trust me on this. She's serious. I would rather she was with you than I was at this point. Alice won't let anything happen to you."

Sydney shrugged. "Sounds like she really knows what she's doing."

"She does." He looked at her for a moment. "Are you done stalling?"

Embarrassed he'd seen right through her, she blushed. "I don't know what you mean."

He chuckled, took her hand, and led her into the only room of the house she hadn't investigated, his bedroom. "This is our room," he said. "Look at the drawers I emptied just for you. Your trunk can go in that corner, and there's a wardrobe here that I keep my dress clothes in. Plenty of room for dresses."

"I think it's a very nice room."

He sat on the foot of the bed. "Look how soft the mattress is."

She blushed again. "Maybe you should go so I can get ready for bed."

He stood up and kissed her softly. "Nothing would make me happier."

She waited until he'd shut the door behind him and picked up her carpet bag. The man was...well, he was exactly what she needed. She could feel it.

Once she was in one of the nightgowns she'd brought from home, she found blankets and piled them onto the bed. The more she was covered with, the harder it would be for him to find her.

Finally, she climbed between the sheets, closing her eyes, and waiting for him. It seemed so strange to be in the bed of a man she'd known for only two days, but she didn't think it mattered too terribly much how long she'd known him. She'd be nervous if they'd known one another for three years.

Lewis knocked on the door before entering the room. She didn't answer, so he opened it a bit and peeked in to see if she was ready. After seeing her lying on one side of the bed, he opened the door, turning down the lamp before he started undressing.

Sydney tried not to look in his direction for fear she'd see something she shouldn't by the light of the moon. Was it even late enough to go to sleep? She didn't know, but if they went to bed early, perhaps she'd be able to get out of bed before noon the next day. She was still so tired from her trip.

Lewis slid into bed beside her and propped himself up on one elbow. "Sydney?"

Sydney turned to him, nodding. Remembering every word of what her mother had told her would happen on the wedding night. "The best way to get through it is to just spread your legs, lie back, and let him do what he will. Never act as if you enjoy it, or he will think you are a loose woman."

Lewis stared at her, startled for a moment. "I would never think you're a loose woman!"

She gasped, her hand going to cover her mouth. She hadn't meant to repeat what her mother had said, aloud, to him! "My mother's advice for the wedding night."

"I'd like you to wipe that advice from your mind. We're just going to start by kissing. I want you to enjoy everything we do together, so don't ever worry I'll think you're a loose woman. That couldn't happen."

"I'm sorry! I didn't mean to say it aloud."

"Of course, you didn't. But I'm glad you did. I understand things a little better now."

He ran his hand over the top of the covers, realizing she'd piled as many on top of herself as she possibly could. "You have got to be hot," he said, wondering just where all these blankets had been. How had she found them?

"I am. But I'm supposed to be modest even in bed with you."

"That's just silly. I'm the man who you'll be waking up beside every day for the rest of your life. I'll be the one who makes love with you and who gives you children."

Lewis got out of bed and carefully peeled layer after layer off his new wife. When she was down to just the sheet, he climbed back in with her. "Isn't that cooler?" He'd heard her talk about how hot it was there enough times that he knew she must have been sweating.

"Much." She turned toward him in bed, no longer lying rigidly on her back with her hands fisted beside her. "Am I really allowed to like it?"

"Of course, you are. God made this pleasurable for both man and woman. He wouldn't want you to not enjoy something he made pleasurable, would he?"

"How do you know all of this?" she asked.

"I just do."

"Have you been to Hell's Half Acre?" she asked, suddenly worried he was used to being with painted ladies, and he would be disappointed with her.

"I have not. But I have a father who will answer any question, and a brother who is married, who will do the same." He paused. "Do you know what my father told me while I was waiting for you to change?"

"No, what?" She reached out and touched his bare shoulder, distracted by the sheer size of the muscles there.

He gathered her close. "He told me to treat you as I would want my sisters to be treated."

"Was that good advice?" she asked.

"It was perfect. It told me that I need to be gentle, patient, and slow." He kissed her softly, his hands slowly moving over her back. "And loving. So loving." His lips left a trail of kisses from her lips to her ear. When he softly bit her earlobe, she gasped in surprise.

He chuckled, his hands moving to her breasts and stroking them, trying to make her want him just as much as he wanted her.

A short while later, they lay on their sides facing one another. Both were out of breath.

"That wasn't nearly as bad as I thought it would be," Sydney said.

Lewis groaned. "It was a thousand times better than I thought it would be. I suppose the answer now is to teach you to love it as much as I do."

Her lips quirked. "Are you up for a challenge like that?"

"I guess we're going to find out. Tomorrow night. For now, let's get some sleep." He glanced over at a small table beside the bed where he kept his gun. They'd be safe for the night. He'd have to sleep with one eye open.

Contrary to Lewis, Sydney was asleep as soon as her eyes were closed, and she slept like a rock. She had no need to worry. Lewis would protect her from whatever came her way.

Lewis watched her sleep, praying he'd have time to nap the following day while Sydney was with Alice.

Chapter Nine

To her surprise, Sydney woke early the following morning, and dressed before Lewis was even awake.

She had no idea what to do, though, because the house was clean and there was no food to cook. She sat for a short while before Lewis woke and walked into the kitchen, where she was sitting at the table.

"What are you doing in here?" he asked.

Sydney shrugged. "I don't know what I'm supposed to do. I thought about cleaning, but your sisters did that last night. I thought about cooking, but there's no food to cook. What exactly am I supposed to do?"

He smiled. "What did you do in your free time in Beckham?"

"I scandalized my mother and the neighbors by biking everywhere in my bloomers."

He couldn't help but laugh at that. "Nothing else?"

"I spent time with the orphans. I volunteered there for three years before I left."

"That's good," he said. "Well, I think what we should do today is head over to Susan and Pa's house for breakfast, and I'll leave you there for the day. I don't want you outside by yourself at all. If I'm not with you, and Alice can't be by your side, then I want you staying in the house."

She pouted. "I don't want to be stuck inside all the time. How will I start a garden if I can't walk outside?"

"You can start a garden next week. For now, we need to make sure you're not found by those men who want to take you back to Massachusetts."

"I guess that makes sense. All right, let me gather everything I want to take to Susan's for us to sew today."

It only took a minute for Sydney to be ready to leave. "I have everything," she told him, standing beside the table.

"Let's go then." She watched as he took a pistol from the table beside the bed and tucked it into the waistband of his pants.

As the two of them walked to Susan's, he held her hand, and talked about what she would like to be purchased so she could cook. "Having looked through all of your cabinets, I realize there is nothing to cook with. Nothing to eat from. You have no pots, no pans, no dishes..."

"Those things will have to go on the list then, won't they?" Lewis asked reasonably.

"But...why have a kitchen if you don't have any of those things? And where did the eggs come from?"

Lewis shrugged. "No idea about the eggs. I figured my wife, when I finally found one, would want to choose pots, pans, and dishes. What if I got a kind she didn't like? I thought it best to wait."

Sydney nodded. At least he could explain his lack of belongings. She only wished she had some idea of why he had breakfast foods with no pans to cook them in. Where had they come from?

When they reached the big house, Sydney went inside to find Mrs. Hackenschleimer already putting breakfast on the table. "I was hoping I could help you cook!" Sydney said.

Mrs. Hackenschleimer shook her head. "Susan is allowed to help with lunch and supper on occasion, but the kitchen is mine for breakfast."

Sydney looked at the food on the table. "What is that anyway?" she asked, as her new family filled in the spots around the table.

"Potato pancakes and bacon," Lewis said, smiling at Mrs. Hackenschleimer. "You're my favorite person in the whole wide world."

Sydney looked at Mrs. Hackenschleimer. "I think I'm going to need your receipt for potato pancakes."

The woman grinned at her. "You are a wise woman."

Lewis had already filled his plate and was doctoring his potato pancake. She watched as he added butter and a little pepper. Then she did the same to her own. Before she had her pancake fixed, she realized the entire family was sitting around the table.

David called for attention before praying. As they ate, he talked with Lewis about how they wanted to handle Sydney for the day. "I don't think she should be outside at all."

Lewis shook his head. "I don't either. I won't mind if she's outside with Alice as long as Alice has her pistol. The rest of the time I want her in the house."

"I agree. I don't think I'd even let her outside with Alice, but it's your decision. Someone should let Alice know to carry her pistol all day." David looked at Thomas. "There's something you can do, Thomas. Run and tell Alice she has to keep the pistol on her today."

Thomas rolled his eyes. "If I drive into Fort Worth, I won't be going to see any of the whores in Hell's Half Acre."

Susan gasped at Thomas's use of the word whore. "You will not use that word at my breakfast table with your younger siblings listening."

Thomas sighed. "Someday I'll do something right."

"Someday!" Susan said, her eyes letting him know she was still angry with him.

"I need to make a shopping list and have someone take it to town and get what we need," Sydney said. "If not, we'll be eating all of our meals here for the foreseeable future."

Susan nodded. "I can send Walter. Or you really can eat all your meals here. We wouldn't mind a bit."

"We all have to eat here on Sundays anyway," Augusta said.

"The whole family you mean?" Sydney asked. She'd had no idea there was a day the entire family would eat together, but she liked the idea.

"Yes," Augusta said. "Ma says we need to act like a family at least once a week, and she chooses Sunday."

Sydney smiled at that. "Well, then I will surely try to act like a family on Sundays."

"Ma will like that," Walter agreed. "If you want to make me a list of things to buy, I'm happy to do it."

"Thanks, Walter."

Thomas made a face but kept his head down and ate his breakfast.

When most of the men left for the day, Lewis lingered. "I don't want to leave before Alice is here," he said.

Susan nodded. "I agree. Where is that girl and her pistol?"

Alice walked in a moment later, her gun visible in her apron pocket, and Rachel in her arms. "I'm here. Go to work, Lewis!"

Lewis kissed Sydney, realizing they would be separated for the first time as a married couple. "Stay safe today. Don't take any risks."

"You act like someone is out to kill me? They just want to take me home to my parents." Sydney sighed. It was going to be a long few days until she felt safe again.

As soon as Lewis was gone, Susan and Alice sat down with Sydney. "Let's make that list of supplies for you," Susan said.

Between the three of them, they were able to list everything Sydney would need before she could start cooking in the little house she shared with Lewis.

"I still don't know why that boy didn't get pots, pans, and dishes when I bought them for Albert," Susan said after they'd finished up. "I offered."

Sydney grinned. "I think he was afraid someone would expect him to cook if he had them."

Alice nodded emphatically. "She's right, Susan. He didn't want anyone thinking he should start feeding himself."

Susan shook her head. "The boy is a mess." She stood up. "Let's move into the parlor with our sewing. Send Rachel up to play with

Clarissa," she suggested. "I think we'll get more done if Rachel isn't clinging to all of our skirts."

Alice told her daughter to go upstairs and play with her aunt. "You can go up by yourself now," she said. "You're a big girl."

It took a little persuasion, but Rachel finally climbed the stairs and waved at her mother from the top.

The three women went into the parlor, and Sydney pulled out the pattern she had found before leaving Massachusetts. Without speaking, they all laid out the pattern pieces on the fabric, and Sydney took the scissors and started cutting.

Alice gasped. "She's doing it with so much confidence!"

"Like she's not worried at all about cutting the wrong thing!" Susan responded.

Sydney looked at the two sisters, frowning. "Is there something you're not telling me?"

Alice shrugged. "We're both afraid to cut. We don't mind sewing, but cutting the fabric is the hard part."

"I see..." Sydney wasn't sure why they were afraid of the initial cuts, but she'd never had a problem making them. She couldn't help but wonder if it was because they had both been raised in poverty, and she had always known more fabric could be purchased.

Either way, she had all three dresses cut out before lunchtime, and each of them began the work of stitching one of them. Susan used her sewing machine, and she finished quickly.

After a quick lunch break of peanut butter and jelly sandwiches, Susan took on the dress Sydney had been sewing so Sydney could cut out a couple of nightgowns. It seemed that each time she finished cutting something, Susan was there to take it from her and work on it.

Two ladies joined them just after two, and they immediately sat down and took pieces that had been cut and started sewing. No explanations were needed about which pieces should be sewn to one another because they'd all been sewing for years.

Susan introduced her friends to her new daughter-in-law. "Wilma, Beverly, this is my new daughter-in-law, Sydney. She married Lewis last night."

"I thought we were coming to make clothes before the wedding!" Beverly said, looking surprised.

"Oh, we were," Wilma said. "Now you have to tell us why you married so quickly."

Sydney took a deep breath. "I came here to escape my mother and her constant attempts to force me to marry a man who was rich and came from old money. My mother was insistent no other man was worthy of our family. I went to Susan and Alice's sister, Elizabeth, and asked to be sent to marry. I got here, only to discover I was supposed to either marry Randy Ranch, or work at Randy's Ranch, and I was willing to do neither. As soon as I found out he owned a brothel, where he spent the majority of his time, I knew I didn't want to marry him. And I certainly didn't want to work for him!"

Wilma let out a giggle. "I shouldn't laugh, but I can just see that happening. Oh, how glad I am you didn't go to work for him and married Lewis instead. Lewis has always been my favorite of the four older Dailey boys."

Sydney smiled. "And why's that?"

"I don't really know. He was just always willing to help me with little projects I needed done, and he always showed me respect."

"Sounds like a good reason to like him best," Sydney said. She cut out the last two things she wanted to make that day, two aprons, and then she sat down with one of them. There were multiple projects cut and waiting to be sewn, even though Susan was hurrying through each project as quickly as her feet could move the treadle.

While they talked, they all laughed about different things, but when a loud knock sounded at the front door, Sydney hurried to the bathroom to hide, while Susan went to the door.

Maybe she should just admit she was there, but she would rather be in the family way before her parents' men found her.

Susan knocked on the bathroom door to let her know it was safe to come out. "It was them, and I told them we had never heard of you. I don't mind fibbing if it's for a really good reason, and protecting you is a good reason."

Sydney returned to the parlor with Susan, only to have Wilma look at her for a moment. "I'm not sure you told the whole story," she said.

"Oh! Yes, my parents seem to have sent someone to look for me and take me back to Beckham. I would rather not go, so I'm hiding so they don't find me. I'm sure they'll realize I'm here eventually, but by then I plan to be expecting."

Beverly laughed. "You really have this figured out, don't you?"

"I try," Sydney said. "My mother won't want me back when she realizes I'm not a virgin anymore. I won't be as easy to marry off that way."

"Oh, dear!" Wilma said, shaking her head. "We won't tell a soul you're here. Those men did come by my house yesterday, but as I hadn't learned your name yet, I very honestly told them I had no idea who you are."

"I'm hoping they move on to the next town, but until then, I'm hiding. I'm not supposed to go outside without Alice and her gun, either."

"That's really smart," Beverly said. "You wouldn't want to risk being snatched up and taken back to Massachusetts, and Alice is a wonderful shot. I've seen her at it, and she's really good!"

Sydney grinned at her friend. Alice must really have impressed a great deal of people with her shooting.

Chapter Ten

When Lewis walked into the big house at the end of the day, Sydney had three mostly completed dresses, two aprons, curtains, pillows, a tablecloth, and two nightgowns cut out, but not sewn yet. It had been an amazing day with fun and laughter despite the men knocking on the door in the middle of their party.

"Walter is back with supplies. He's unloading them onto the table and work table, and you'll need to put them away from there."

She nodded. "That sounds good."

He kissed her. "I think we eat with the family tonight, though. There's safety in numbers."

As much as Sydney wanted to disagree with him so they could start their life separately from his family, she knew he was right. "Did you see the men today?" she asked.

"No, I think they must have moved on."

"They came here. I hid in the bathroom while Susan lied through her teeth."

Lewis frowned. "Good for Susan."

Mrs. Hackenschleimer called from the dining room that supper was served. They all moved to the table, and Sydney was sad to see roast beef. It was her favorite meat in Beckham, but she was enjoying chicken so much, it felt strange to not have it for a meal.

Of course the meal was delicious. Mrs. Hackenschleimer wouldn't serve anything less. She observed the family as she ate, enjoying how the siblings spoke to one another. She never would have known all the children hadn't had the same two parents if she hadn't already been told.

The twins—both sets—argued good-naturedly with one another. Lewis just gazed at her as if she was a priceless painting, while Susan fed little Clarissa. The whole scene was crazy to her, but also wonderful. Every time she was with this family, she realized again how much she had missed out on by being an only child.

When supper was over, David, Walter, and Thomas, all agreed to walk her home along with Lewis. "Do I really need that many people watching out for me? It doesn't sound like these men are dangerous!" Sydney protested.

Lewis shrugged sheepishly. "I'm afraid they'll turn dangerous when they realize you're already married."

"Perhaps," she said, shrugging. "I have no idea who they are."

Once they were inside their house, David, Walter, and Thomas all went back to their own home, and Sydney couldn't help but wonder if they would all be there in the morning to guard her. The whole thing just seemed like a mess to her.

By Saturday night, she still hadn't cooked a single meal in her own home. She was guarded too well to do anything but go where she was told. It was worse than living with her mother. She had no choice about where she put her feet, let alone be able to ride her bicycle, even for a short while.

They had talked about going to the church social, but at the last minute, Lewis declared it was too dangerous.

Sydney had enough. "I'm going to put on my prettiest dancing dress, and I'm going to the church social with you. I'll be safe, and you'll be beside me the whole time." She shut the bedroom door in Lewis's face and dressed for the evening.

Lewis hurried to his parents' house and let them know what was happening, so everyone could be there to watch his bride. Why were women so difficult when you needed them to behave?

Lewis decided to make the night as wonderful for her as he could, and he hitched up one of the courting buggies with his favorite team that had been both bred and trained there at the ranch. When Sydney came out of their bedroom, she wore a beautiful pink dress that was off her shoulders. He stopped where he was and nodded to her. "You look beautiful."

Sydney smiled and walked to him, linking her hands at the back of his neck. "Am I dressed all right for the social?" she asked.

He swallowed hard. It was still difficult to believe she was his wife, and he'd be the one taking her home at the end of the night. "I think you're a bit fancier than the other ladies will be, but you will definitely be the belle of the ball!"

"Fancy works for me. I'm tired of being cooped up. Tonight, I want to meet all your friends. I hope there's dancing because I want to spend the night dancing in your arms under the light of the moon."

He grinned. Maybe he had gone a little overboard with trying to keep her safe.

He offered her his arm, and they walked out to the buggy together, and he handed her up, and made sure she was settled in her half of the conveyance.

The whole way to the church, Sydney talked about how freeing it was to finally go somewhere other than his parents' house. "You just don't understand. I feel like I've been locked away my entire life, and I was waiting for my life to start. Sure, I'd get a few hours here and there on my bicycle, or with the orphans, but I truly felt life was passing me by. And then when I was hiding here, it was just as bad." She shook her head. "I can't be locked away anymore."

Lewis covered her hand with his own. "I'm sorry I made you feel that way."

"I know you're just trying to protect me, but I don't think the men will hurt me. My parents want me back safe and sound, not in a hearse."

At the church, he helped her to her feet, and led her to where the pastor stood by himself. "Are you still missing your wife, Pastor?" she asked sweetly.

The man nodded. "I am. But she'll be home next week, and then I'll wonder when she's going to visit her mother again."

Sydney laughed. "I think that's how it should be."

"I do too. Have you enjoyed your time here, Mrs. Dailey?"

It was the first time the name had been applied to her and she stopped for a moment. "I have. The Dailey family has been warm and welcoming. I really like them all so much, and Susan has treated me like a new daughter."

"That's Susan. I'm not sure David realizes just what a prize he has in her."

Sydney felt a tapping at her shoulder, and when she turned, her heart dropped into her stomach. "Papa."

Her father, a portly man who was slightly shorter than she was herself, opened his arms and she flew into them. "Is Mother here?"

"No, I left her at home because I wasn't going to listen to her nag. I thought you were with the Daileys, but every time I asked, they said they'd never heard of you. But I recognized that bicycle of yours."

Sydney laughed. "I guess we should have hidden that away in the carriage house."

"It would have helped your cause, I think."

"Why are you here, Papa?"

"I want to make sure you're all right. You didn't come here to marry into the Dailey family, did you?"

Sydney sighed. "I didn't. But before I left Beckham, Elizabeth told me of her sister living here and what her name was. When I realized the error I'd made coming out here, I got directions to Susan Dailey's house, and I rode my bike out to meet her."

"Are you happy, child?" Her father looked deeply into her eyes as if he was trying to read her soul.

Sydney felt Lewis walk up behind her and he gave her strength. "I am. I was never going to be happy with one of the men Mother kept trying to force me upon. Here, I can be myself, and I can wear bloomers and ride my bicycle whenever I want."

Her father nodded. "And this man you married? Is he good to you?"

"He is. He makes me feel like I'm cherished and loved more than any woman deserves to be loved."

"Introduce me to him."

Sydney was still nervous as she turned so she could see Lewis. "Papa, this is my husband, Lewis Dailey. Lewis, this is my father, Edmond Weatherby."

Lewis held his hand out for the older man to shake. "It's good to meet you, Mr. Weatherby."

Her papa looked Lewis up and down for a moment before shaking his hand. "It's good to meet you. My daughter says you're good to her. I had better never hear you have treated her poorly."

Lewis put his arm around Sydney, still feeling the need to protect her. "You will not hear I've been rude or unkind to her. I'm in love with your daughter, sir, and I plan to follow the advice my father gave me on my wedding day."

"What advice is that?"

"I'll treat her as I want my sisters to be treated when they marry."

Edmond smiled, nodding slightly. "Then you are the son-in-law I've been hoping for."

"You won't make me go home, Papa?" Sydney asked, still not sure exactly what was going on.

"I won't. I will explain to your mother you're happily married. She'd love a visit from you when you can, but she won't be putting any kind of pressure on you ever again."

Sydney threw herself at her father, hugging him close. "Thank you! Tell Mother I love her."

"I will. Now, introduce me to the rest of this big family you married into."

Sydney hurried around, introducing her father to each of the Daileys. She even introduced him to Clarissa and little Rachel.

"And you're going to have a large family, I presume?"

Sydney shrugged. "I'll have as many children as God wants me to have."

"We want at least a dozen, sir." Lewis hadn't been more than a step or two away from her the entire evening.

"A dozen?" Her papa chuckled. "Your mother is going to want one of them to marry well. Her idea of well, not ours." He winked at Sydney.

She smiled. "I'll make sure at least one marries well." Her idea of well, not her mother's. She knew her papa understood that.

"I'm going to take my leave," Papa told her. "I need to get back to your mother who I'm certain has paced a trench in the floor in the blue parlor."

"I'm certain she has." Once again she embraced her father. "Thank you for coming to make sure I'm safe, Papa."

"I've been a day behind you the entire way. I did lose you for a moment when I got to Fort Worth, but then I talked to a woman who told me she gave you directions to the Daileys'. It was easy from there."

As her father walked to his rented carriage, Sydney sighed. She would miss him, but she was in a much better position now.

Lewis held his hand out for the first dance of the evening, and as soon as they were waltzing in the middle of the church lawn, she asked, "Did I hear you tell my papa that you love me?"

Lewis swallowed hard. "Yes, you did. And I'm not even ashamed of it."

"Ashamed of lying to him? Or ashamed of telling him the truth?"

"I do love you, Sydney. God was certainly smiling down on me when you rode your bicycle to the ranch and befriended my mother."

"No, he was smiling on me." She rested her head on his shoulder for just a moment. "I love you too, Lewis Dailey. With everything inside of me."

He kissed her and when he lifted his head, there was a slight grin on his face. "Does that mean you'll teach me to ride your bike tomorrow?"

"I will, but wouldn't it be more fun if you had one of your own?"

"Let's make sure I don't kill myself on the thing first!" he said, realizing that his life was just now beginning. With Sydney.

Epilogue

Sydney sat in the gazebo with Susan and Alice and Alice's new twins. Susan's waist was thick with the baby she was carrying. "Maybe you'll have twins again as well!" Alice said.

"Bite your tongue! Raising two sets of twins is enough for anyone."

"I suppose," Alice said, grinning at her sister.

Sydney smiled as she watched them, playing with Rachel as she hurried around the gazebo. "I can safely say me too."

Susan frowned at her. "You too, what?"

"You're going to be a grandmother again, Susan."

Susan laughed. "And I'll have a child right around my grandchildren's age. I think Sydney should be the one to have twins."

"Why me?" Sydney asked.

"Because Lewis needs to figure out how to deal with them."

Sydney laughed. "But then I'd have to deal with them too!"

Later that evening, she was sitting with Lewis as they ate their supper. "This is really good!" he said of her first attempt to make fried chicken.

"Of course it is. It's Mrs. H's receipt."

"No surprise there," he said, taking another piece. "Aren't you going to eat more?"

She shook her head. "No, I'm a bit queasy this evening."

"Do you need to see a doctor?"

"No, it's nothing that won't work itself out in about eight months..."

Lewis stood up and pulled her to her feet, holding her close. "We're having a baby!"

"And not two," Sydney said.

"Huh?"
"I'll explain later. I love you, Lewis."
"And I love you, Sydney."

SIGN UP FOR INSTANT notification of all of Kirsten's New Releases Text 'BOB' to 42828

Don't miss out!

Visit the website below and you can sign up to receive emails whenever Kirsten Osbourne publishes a new book. There's no charge and no obligation.

https://books2read.com/r/B-A-VSFD-LWBZB

BOOKS 2 READ

Connecting independent readers to independent writers.

www.ingramcontent.com/pod-product-compliance
Lightning Source LLC
LaVergne TN
LVHW092336171025
823772LV00034B/316